Lunatics

Based on the Life of Judith Love Cohen
Written by
Elyse Wilk

ASIN: 1481084194
ISBN: 9781481084192

To Harvey Wilk, my husband and best friend.

Thank you for your patience and eternal optimism!

A special thanks to the late Ingenious Judith Love Cohen,

her husband David Katz and to her many inspirations, the

late Bernard Siegel, Neil Siegel, Rachel Siegel, The late

Howard Siegel, Thomas Jacob Black, all their life partners

and her grandchildren.

MATH IS SEXY AND NUMBERS DON'T LIE

Table of Contents

Chapter One 1

Chapter Two 15

Chapter Three 27

Chapter Four 41

Chapter Five..54

Chapter Six 62

Chapter Seven...75

Chapter Eight...82

Chapter Nine...91

Chapter Ten 100

Chapter Eleven...108

Chapter Twelve...115

Chapter Thirteen 122

Chapter Fourteen 130

Part Two...143

Chapter Fifteen 145

Chapter Sixteen..156

Chapter Seventeen 163

chapter Eighteen 177

Chapter Nineteen 187

Chapter Twenty 201

Chapter Twenty-one 208

chapter Twenty-two 213

Chapter Twenty-three 238

Chapter Twenty-four 248

Chapter Twenty-five.....................................260

Chapter Twenty-six 265

Chapter Twenty-seven...................................271

Chapter Twenty-eight 278

Chapter Twenty-Nine 292

Chapter Thirty...297

Chapter Thirty-one..306

Part Three...319

Chapter Thirty-two 321

Chapter Thirty-three 337

chapter Thirty-four..349

Chapter Thirty-five 356

ABOUT THE AUTHOR 367

CHAPTER ONE

The year is 1951.

Standing center stage with her back to the audience, in the darkened high school auditorium, is Mrs. Temple, the conductor. She's wearing her special little black dress, except she isn't little anymore, it's well-worn, and a bit too tight, so as she raises her conductor's baton the flab under her arms jiggles like Jell-O when she taps the top of her music stand to get the choir's attention, then she powerfully points it at the sopranos and the Lafayette High School Holiday Musical Program is underway.

As their voices fill the room everyone quiets down apart from a couple of dry coughs. At the precise instant before Mrs. Temple motions with her stubby index finger for the altos to join in, she forcefully pushes her heavy horn-rimmed glasses up her large, crooked nose.

Julie stands facing her from the center of the chorus wearing a festive white choral gown. She feels especially uncomfortable with the song selection and takes a deep breath before she squeaks out the first note of Silent Night knowing how much it will upset her father. She grips her Star of David between her thumb and index finger and imagines how much he will grumble about it after the performance.

The show ends with a great round of applause for the chorus's big number Rudolf the Red Nosed Reindeer. Julie navigates through a sea of people pushing their way toward the exit doors. When she finally reaches her parents, her father greets her with a scowl on his face. Her mother nervously assists Julie with her dark wool coat while pretending everything is all right. Julie looks into her mother's-tired eyes and tries to grasp what she was attempting to communicate – it's despair.

Julie remains quiet while her father rants, "That was meshuga, and you shouldn't be singing about such things!"

Julie knows better than to argue with her father when he's angry, so she nods her head in agreement and assures herself it will pass quickly because he is a sweet and kind person. Meanwhile, to make things worse, the high school's principal, Mr. Swartz, swims like a shark through the thinning crowd toward them and comes over to speak directly with Julie's father. Mr. Swartz always makes Julie feel terribly uncomfortable and she can feel knots forming in her stomach as he approaches them.

"Thank goodness I caught up with you, Mr. Levine." Mr. Swartz straightens his ridiculous candy-cane-colored holiday tie. The tie has an absurdly placed, off-center, holiday tiepin, as if Mr. Swartz is trying to conceal a food stain, but all the tiepin does is point to where it is and brings more attention to it.

Julie's father sounds terrified when he asks Mr. Swartz in an almost inaudible whisper, "My Julie, she isn't in any kind of trouble is she?"

Mr. Swartz loudly exclaims, "No, of course not, but there is something important we need to discuss. When can you come into my office to see me?"

Mr. Levine swallows before he answers him, "Day after tomorrow, if that's all right with you, Mr. Swartz."

Mr. Swartz sees he's upset Julie's father and tries to be helpful when he coaxes him with, "Mr. Levine, I appreciate that it's difficult to take time off, especially right before Christmas."

"I can come at 7 in the morning, if that meets with your approval?" He doesn't dare inquire again into what this matter is about in fear Mr. Swartz might reveal something of an embarrassing nature in his overly loud voice while they are standing in the middle of a crowded public space.

Mr. Swartz offers no more information on the subject and simply confirms the appointment with him, "That's fine, Mr. Levine, I'll see you then."

#

During the ride home on the subway, Julie sits between her parents. Her head rests on her mother's slumped over shoulder when her father startles her with the beginnings of his inquisition. "What did you do?"

Julie simply shrugs to express that she has no idea. Her father angrily proclaims, "Well then, why don't you recite the Fibonacci numbers for me until we reach our stop!"

Julie protests, "Pop, I could be up into the millions by then, and I'm tired."

Her father says in a stern voice, "Julie."

Unenthusiastically, she begins to add the numbers together in her head and recite the answers aloud, "0 plus 1 is 1, 1 plus 2 is 3, 2 plus 3 is 5, 3 plus 5 is 8, 5 plus 3 is 8,

Her father interrupts, "You repeated yourself."

She nods and continues, "8 plus 5 is 13, 8 plus 13 is 21, 13 plus 21 is 34, 21 plus 34 is 55, 34 plus 55 is 89, 55 plus 89 is 144, 89 plus 144 is 233, 144 plus 233 is 377, 233 plus 377 is 610, 377 plus 610 is 987, 610 plus 987 is 1,597, 987 plus 1,597 is 2,584, 1,597 plus 2,584 is 4,181, 2,584 plus 4,181 is 6,765."

Julie's father interrupts her again, "Look, we're at Flatbush already, and you didn't even reach five figures."

#

After the brisk walk from the station, Julie feels sandwiched between her parents in their tiny, rickety elevator with its retractable gold metal grate. As they pass by each floor on the way up to their apartment, a waft of different-smelling ethnic foods presses in upon them. When they reach their floor, her father opens the grate to the elevator door as he erupts into another tirade, "I have to meet with the principal, and you have no idea why?"

Julie's mother finally comes to her daughter's defense, "Quiet, the neighbors will hear."

Julie's mother knocks on their next-door neighbor's door. Julie and her father stand behind her mother while Julie complains under her breath about the terrible stink emanating from the apartment and says with a smirk, "I think Mrs. Linsky burnt her brisket."

Julie's mother knocks on the door again, this time a little louder because Mrs. Linsky is a bit hard of hearing. Instantaneously, Julie's father turns and shouts in his daughter's face while he points his index finger at her. "That's it, isn't it? You were a smart aleck!"

Just then Mrs. Linsky opens her apartment door and Rose, Julie's baby sister, scoots into the hallway. Julie's mother says courteously, "Thank you, Mrs. Linsky, for taking care of Rose for us tonight."

Mrs. Linsky responds while drying her rough, chapped hands on her faded-flowered housedress, "She complained that she wasn't very hungry and pecked at her dinner like a little bird. I would check her temperature when you put her to bed."

Julie's mother replies defensively, "I'm sorry she was such a burden."

Later that same evening Rose and Julie are dressed in their nightgowns and feeling warm under their covers. Rose rolls over to poke her sister in the ribs, "Julie, I want you to sneak into the kitchen and get me something to eat. I'm too short to reach it, so go look in the high cabinet first, that's where Mama usually hides her strudel."

Julie snickers, "Didn't you have dinner at Mrs. Linsky's house?"

Julie's question infuriates Rose, and she whines,
"You're kidding me, even a dog would starve over there.
Now, get me strudel!"

"I can't, I'm already in enough trouble, go to sleep!"

This news shocks Rose, and she questions her sister,
"You, Papa's little miss perfect, you're in trouble! What
did you do?" Then she smiles.

"I don't have a clue, now go to sleep!" Julie states as if
it's a command.

Rose is intrigued and continues to badger her older sister
for information. "So, why do you think you're in trouble?"

"Pop has to meet with Mr. Swartz, the school's
principal."

"That's sounds really bad." Rose pats her sister on the
back to comfort her and then rolls over and tries to fall
asleep while her empty stomach grumbles.

#

Julie's father arrives early for his 7 a.m. meeting at the principal's office. Mr. Swartz is already at work at his desk when he notices Mr. Levine standing outside waiting for an invitation to enter. He motions for him to come in and take a seat. Mr. Levine keeps his heavy coat on in the hope that the meeting will be short, but he removes his hat out of respect. Then he sits still and remains silent while he watches Mr. Swartz enjoy his pipe.

Mr. Swartz exhales a large puff before he speaks. "Mr. Levine, thank you for coming in this morning to see me."

Mr. Levine fidgets in his seat and says nothing. Mr. Swartz stares at him while he mechanically refills his pipe with tobacco. Mr. Levine begins to sweat, and regrets not taking the time to take off his heavy overcoat.

Mr. Swartz waves his pipe around with flourish while he speaks. "Mr. Levine, your daughter Julie is… how should I put this? Well… she's quite the most unusual young lady."

"I beg your pardon. My wife and I have always thought of Julie as being a normal little girl, she goes to band practice, as well as ballet, and she receives excellent marks on her report cards."

Mr. Swartz sits straight up in his chair while he expands on his last observation. "She is normal, but you see someone gave her the crazy notion that she should apply for the college preparatory classes."

Mr. Levine appears culpable, as he looks down at his shoes and twists the rim of his hat in his sweaty palms.

Mr. Swartz assumes that Mr. Levine has no idea what he was talking about, so he offers, "Don't worry, Mr. Levine, I'll get right to the bottom of it and find out which teacher is encouraging her with this silly and delusional idea."

"Then what happens?" Mr. Levine inquires.

"I'll compose a strongly written reprimand and make sure that the high school's policy is strictly enforced."

Mr. Swartz's statement infuriates him, so he shakes his head negatively in response to it, as he feels his body heat building up and his temper rise. That's when he unbuttons the last button and leans in to speak frankly, but at that exact same moment Mr. Swartz exhales another large puff of pipe smoke directly in his face. Mr. Levine feels exasperated, and he holds nothing back. "Mr. Swartz, I'm the person responsible for giving Julie those ambitious ideas."

Mr. Swartz is surprised, "You know that it goes against everything we recommend and will inevitably lead your daughter down the wrong path."

English is Mr. Levine's third language, and when he's upset, he often forgets the words he wants to use, so he does his best to explain his actions, "I make a meager living, Mr. Swartz. Therefore, I can't afford to send my girls away to a fancy, expensive college, so encouragement is all that I've got to give them."

"Mr. Levine, that's exactly the reason why we offer so many excellent courses that teach our young lady's useful skills, such as how to type, cook, and sew."

Mr. Levine shakes his head again. "I think you have my daughter confused with another student."

Mr. Swartz argued, "I appreciate she's exceptionally bright, but I think you need to decide what is best for your daughter in the long term."

"So, what you're telling me is my daughter will not be permitted to join the college preparatory class."

"That's correct; I'm not going against the school's age-old policy."

Mr. Levine protests, "Well, why not?"

Mr. Swartz angrily waves his pipe while he expounds, "Because it will distract the boys from their studies."

Mr. Levine is disgusted with his explanation and losses his self-control, "That's ridiculous!"

"Mr. Levine, I wish you could see this my way." Then he adds more tobacco to his pipe and lights it up again, as Mr. Levine pleads, "Mr. Swartz, you're asking me to apologize to you for raising my girls to use their brains."

"If you were the father of a son, you'd see things differently, Mr. Levine. Trust me, I am the expert here."

Feeling defeated, Mr. Levine asks, "What do you want from me, Mr. Swartz?"

"Encourage Julie to do more things with her mother around the house and make sure to sign her up for home economics or an elocution class next semester."

Mr. Levine responds sarcastically, "And you think that will help?"

"God willing, Mr. Levine. My only hope is I've intervened in enough time so that she'll be able to get married someday to a nice boy and have a family."

CHAPTER TWO

Julie sits down at a cafeteria table without uttering a word

to the three attractive, older boys already seated there.

They're busy at work and struggling with their math

homework. They don't even bother to look up at her. She

slowly unpacks her school bag. She reveals an egg salad

sandwich on white bread and a plaid thermos full of milk.

As she reaches back down to the bottom of the bag, she

realizes all three of them are staring at her with the same intense expression of anxiety. She ignores them as she pulls out a protractor, slide rule, and a couple of pencils. Then she grasps the thick math textbook in the middle of the table and turns it around to see which problems they are working on. After she reviews it, she says, "Okay, let me see your answers."

They reluctantly hand over their small blue workbooks. Julie examines Larry's answer first. "Wow, you're making progress. This is pretty darn close, but you put the decimal in the wrong place."

Larry flashes a quick smile at her, and then he immediately returns to his expressionless stone-face. She likes Larry a lot and wished sometimes that he wasn't so bashful. She takes a good look at him and thinks that if he didn't comb his hair sideways and hadn't globed on so much pomade, he could be somewhat cute, despite his dark, thick unibrow. She picks up her eraser, fixes his answer, and returns the workbook to him with a barely audible sigh.

After that, Julie reaches for Bill's workbook, as he appears to gloat because he feels confident, he has the correct answer. After she peruses his workbook, she looks into his big blue eyes and says, "The answer is a negative number, not a positive one, Einstein." Immediately Bill's ego appears deflated. When he takes back his corrected math homework from Julie, he still can't believe a girl who wasn't old enough to be in his class is tutoring him. That isn't even the worst part about it; he also knows in his heart that he can't get a good grade in math without her help.

Julie is so engrossed with Bill that she doesn't notice Betty Ann Abramowitz has come over to their table and is distracting the boys with her voluptuously filled low-cut, tight, yellow cashmere sweater. Betty Ann seems most interested in Henry. Unfortunately for him, he is also the boy who needs the most help from Julie.

Betty Ann makes no eye contact with Julie when she speaks to everyone at the table and asks, "What are you boys doing?"

Julie's blood begins to boil, and she is dismayed at the change in the boys' expressions from studious to stupid. She couldn't believe how ignorantly Betty Ann treats her and doesn't understand why she said, "You boys," ignoring Julie's presence altogether. Julie feels as if time has stopped while Betty Ann continues to allow the boys to admire her cleavage as she sways it back and forth for them. Julie examines Betty Ann more closely and recalls from the girls' locker room what is underneath that tight yellow sweater, as it's wads of balled up toilet paper instead of the flesh the boys at her table are imagining.

Henry makes an earnest attempt at impressing Betty Ann. "We're working on our calculus homework." Then he turns the textbook around for her to see the math problem.

Betty Ann glances down at the page and then looks deeply into Henry's eyes before she replies, "Looks real hard," and then she batts her long eyelashes.

Her comment makes Julie feel as if she's going to vomit up her lunch into her mouth, so she retorts, "It's just math, Betty Ann, and any knucklehead who studies can do it."

Betty Ann sneers at Julie.

It appears Henry does not want Betty Ann to know that he requires Julie's help, so desperately he tries to conceal what is really taking place at the cafeteria table that day. "Betty Ann, Julie is catching on to it so nicely too. Aren't you, Julie?"

His comment makes Julie hysterical, "What do you mean, I've been …"

Henry swiftly kicks Julie from under the table and glares at her while his face reddens. Then he turns his attention to Betty Ann, "What are you doing this coming Saturday night?"

Betty Ann sways her body back and forth again when she states coyly, "I hope I'm going out with you, Henry."

"Great, I'll pick you up at 7. There's a party at Sally's."

Betty Ann smiles victoriously and then walks over to a table full of girls dressed just like her, also with matching wads of toilet paper stuffed in their brassieres. Although the girls are sitting on the opposite side of the cafeteria, they have been observing Betty Ann the entire time she's visiting Julie's study table.

Julie attempts to refocus the group. "What was that all about?"

Henry says sarcastically, "Something, you'll never understand."

Julie is disgusted with Henry's behavior. She reaches for his math workbook and looks at it. "Your answer isn't even close."

Henry flirtatiously flutters his long eyelashes just like Betty Ann did and pleads, "You're still gunna help me, aren't you?"

She is still incensed over his earlier comment and replies, "Why don't you ask Betty Ann to figure it out for you?" After that she tosses the workbook at him, and he catches it right before it hits him.

Just then Mrs. Temple, who is in addition to the choral conductor is also the boys AP math teacher, reaches their table. The boys sit up straighter as she addresses Julie and points to her, "Please come with me, we need to talk in private."

Julie finds this situation incredulous and nervously asks, "Do you mean me?" While she taps herself on her chest with her slide rule.

"Yes, Julie, and right now, I don't have a lot of time before my next class starts."

From across the room Julie could see Betty Ann gloating as she followed Mrs. Temple out of the cafeteria with her head hung low. In the reflection of the large glass panes of the cafeteria doors, Julie watches Betty Ann whisper something into the ear of Fanny Gold, and she in turn whispers something into the ear of the next girl. At that moment, Julie feels so humiliated she wishes she could make herself vanish.

#

Mrs. Temple doesn't say a word to Julie in the bustling hallway. Julie follows her into the empty classroom, and Mrs. Temple points to a seat in the middle of the first row and tells her to take seat. Mrs. Temple stands over Julie while leaning against the front of her big oak desk. Just as she is about to speak, she hesitates and decides to walk over to the open classroom door and close it first. When she returns, she faces Julie and says, "I just came from Mr. Swartz's office. He instructed me to fill your head with ideas about what it means to be a girl in today's modern world and encourage you to go to finishing school where they will turn you into a proper young lady."

Julie's eyes swell with tears, "Mrs. Temple, did I do something wrong?"

"No, you didn't, sweetheart."

Julie is feeling frustrated and confused, "Then why am I here?"

Mrs. Temple tries to explain as best she can, but there seems to be a strain in her voice when she speaks. "You've reached an important fork in the road, and I want to make sure you go in the right direction."

Julie is confused and confesses, "I don't understand what you're talking about."

"Julie, it's this. Mr. Swartz will not allow you to join my college prep math class because he says that it's meant only for the boys."

"I see." Julie spontaneously begins to cry. Mrs. Temple hands her a clean handkerchief that it appears she had set aside for this meeting.

Then Mrs. Temple continues, "You're my star pupil, and I'm not ready to give up on you yet." She picks up a thick math book and hands it to Julie. "This is the textbook I use for the college prep class, and I want you to study from it on your own."

Julie sounds defeated, "What's the point? I'll never get credit for taking the class."

"Julie, that's all I can offer you for now. I want you to prepare yourself for the scholarship test. This class isn't at all about getting high school credits. What it's really about is deciding who will get the college scholarship from your graduating class. If you get a high enough score, they'll have to consider you for the scholarship."

Julie wipes away the tears from her red splotchy eyes, picks up the heavy book, and places it in her school bag.

Suddenly and without warning she hugs Mrs. Temple. Mrs.
Temple pats Julie's back while she confides, "We can do
this, but you must keep it our little secret." Julie nods her
head in agreement and then walks out into the busy
hallway. It was jammed with kids rushing to their next
class, and as she pushes her way through, she feels as if she
is a salmon trying to swim upstream.

Just as she reaches her biology class, the school's
guidance counselor steps out in front of her and says,
"Julie, so glad I ran into you. Mr. Swartz asked me to meet
with you, so stop by my office later today. I set aside a
brochure for the perfect finishing school for a girl like
you."

Julie can taste bile in her mouth and has nothing to say
to the guidance counselor as she nods her head yes. She
tries to hide her frustration because she knows this was an
ambush. She turns away and walks even faster to her next
class. She takes her seat and tries to catch her breath. That's

when she comes to the realization that she must pick up

that brochure; otherwise, Mr. Swartz might get wise to

what was going on behind his back.

CHAPTER THREE

Julie's father stands silently in the hallway while he
observes his daughter studying. He decides this is a good
time to have a chat with her, so he quietly sits down on the
end of the bed she shares with her sister Rose. She doesn't
notice him because she's engrossed in her textbook. Her
father gently takes her foot in his hand and shales it to get
her attention. With the sound of concern in his voice, he

asks her a question. "My shayna madela, why are you studying so much on a Saturday night?"

Julie drops the heavy math book and looks up at her father. "I don't know. I've nothing better to do tonight, so why not get a little ahead."

Her father protests, "It's Chanukah. Isn't there a party somewhere, or don't you have some girlfriends you could go to see a movie with?"

"Pop, what's this about?"

"Mr. Swartz told me I've pushed you too hard and given you unrealistic goals."

"I love you, Pop. I like things exactly the way they are, and I wouldn't change a thing."

"I want for you to be happy, get married, and have children someday." Her father reaches in his pocket for his handkerchief and blows his nose into it, then puts it back in his pocket. He conceals from Julie that he's holding back his tears and that he fears Mr. Swartz might have been right about what he said at their meeting.

"Pop, I want those things too, but I also want other things," she protests.

"Like what?" He enjoys listening to his daughter's daydreams, and he smiles while she answers him.

"I want to go away to college, so I can learn about cosmic rays and how to reach escape velocity. That's the only way I'll ever become a rocket scientist and be able to build spaceships that travel around the galaxy."

Her father laughs at her. "That's meshuga; I think you've been reading too many comic books. Now go in the kitchen and help momma."

"All right, Pop." Julie pushes her math book aside and gets up from the bed.

When Julie enters the kitchen, her mother is almost finished putting away the dishes.

"Momma, is there anything you'd like me to do for you?"

Her mother looks around the tiny kitchen and says, "Would you mind taking the big bag of garbage down to the incinerator? It's too large for the chute and Pop wants to read a book."

Julie reaches for it and scowls because it's especially greasy from the potato latkes, and it smells of white fish salad that had been rotting since the morning's breakfast. She walks out to the hall and presses the elevator button. When the door opens, she doesn't realize there is another person in it because the bag blocks her view. She's startled when it lurches up instead of down. She looks at the panel to see if she pushed the wrong button.

That's when the young man in the elevator inquires, "Julie, is that you behind the bag?"

She drops the bag down a couple of inches and sounds confused when she asks, "Larry, what are you doing here?"

"Sally's party is tonight. I can't believe you don't know about it."

Julie sounds hurt when she replies. "She didn't invite me."

"I'm sure it's because it's mostly seniors. Want to come along with me? You can be my sort of a date."

"I need to get rid of this smelly bag of trash and then ask Mama."

"Sure, let me help you with that." The elevator stops at the ninth floor and Julie pushes the button again for the basement. That's when Larry reaches over and takes the bag out of her hands. The elevator arrives in the basement, and they walk over to the ominous hot and blackened incinerator. Larry drops the smelly trash in the barrel, wipes his greasy hands on his pants, and then he comments, "It's warm down here."

Julie smiles at him, and for a brief millisecond, he smiles back at her. She suggests, "Why don't you go to the party, and I'll meet you there in a few minutes?"

Julie rushes back to her apartment and tells her mother she's going up to Sally's but fails to mention the party. She brushes her teeth, washes her face, and changes her blouse.

Just as she is about to dash out, her father stops her. "Where are you going?"

She realizes that telling him the truth would give him some feeling of joy, so she says smugly, "To a party at Sally's."

"Have a nice time," while raising an eyebrow.

#

When the elevator door opens, there are several people already squeezed into it, so Julie lets the door close and runs up the four flights of stairs. She enters the apartment and Sally exclaims, "Julie, I'm so glad you're here." Just as if she had formally invited her. Then she asks her sweetly, "Can you help me in the kitchen?"

A couple of girls are already at work on the food. One of them is Betty Ann Abramowitz. She isn't at all pleased to see Julie. "What are you doing here?" she demands.

"Larry invited me."

"Isn't he swell? I can't figure out for the life of me why Sally invited him because everyone thinks he's such a schlep." Julie ignores Betty Ann's hurtful comment and helps the other girls carry the sandwiches and bottles of soda to the table in the living room. Plus, she's happy to just get away from that horrible Betty Ann.

Larry turns the radio to a swing band station, and the kids start to dance. The remainder of the guests have arrived, and Sally asks Julie to help them with their coats and boots. When the coat pile reaches about five feet high, it dawns on Julie that Sally's mother and father are not at home. At first, she thinks they might have gone across the hall to visit neighbors and are listening from next door. Briefly, she considers leaving, but then decides to stay even though she knows how upset her parents would be if they found out the party wasn't chaperoned. This also titillates her, and what flashes through her mind is that this is going to be a keen party. She feels ecstatic and smiles; even though her invitation was a last second after thought, that only happened because she coincidentally ran into Larry in the elevator on her way to take out the trash.

As the evening wears on, she notices various boys and girls pairing up and going off to secluded dark corners in the apartment to make out. Julie gets up from the sofa to get something to eat and a bottle of soda pop. As soon as she reaches over for a cherry soda, she realizes Larry is standing next to her. He begins to make himself an enormous plate of food. A thick piece of chocolate cake weighs it down on one side, balanced on the other side by a couple of half-sour pickles and a tongue sandwich. He nonchalantly turns to her and asks if she wants to join him at the tiny two-person kitchen table.

After they sit down, he asks her with a mouth full of food, "How come you're so smart?" Then he wipes the mustard from his face with a party napkin.

She giggles, "I'm not. I just work hard at my studies."

He washes down the sandwich before he speaks. "Who are you trying to kid? I'm in your study group. I work hard too, but you already know all the answers."

Julie decides to change the subject because she really doesn't know the answer to that question. Math is a language to her just like English is to everyone else, and she feels as if she was born already fluent in it.

"So, Larry, what do you plan to do after high school?" Julie figures he'll talk for a while, so she takes a big bite out of her chopped liver on rye and begins to chew it.

Larry becomes somber and pensive. "My plan was to go to college and hopefully someday to become a sound engineer." Julie nods affirmatively and continues to munch on her sandwich. "But my dad died last summer from a heart attack, so I've got no choice. I must support my mother and kid brother."

Julie feels a lump form in her throat from his story and puts the sandwich down. She speaks softly, "That's so sad, I knew your father passed away, but it never occurred to me that you'd have to take care of your family."

Larry stares off into space while holding his sandwich over his plate. After that long pause, he continues to share his grief with her. "My mother is an angel and she's smart too, but her English isn't very good. The best she can do is get piecework in a garment factory."

"What if you won a scholarship to college?"

Larry thinks about the question for a moment, "I hope to God I don't and that my baby brother wins one instead of me. Without the money I bring home from my part-time job, my family would end up starving or living on the street,"

There is a moment of silence when they look at each other and recognize their mutual attraction. Larry blushes, takes another sip of his celery soda, and asks, "What about you, kid? What are your plans?"

"Promise you won't laugh at mine."

Larry laughs before he says, "I swear I won't unless it's really funny."

Julie blurts out, "I want to learn how to build rockets and super-sized telescopes and figure out how to travel to outer space." She waits for Larry's response, but he remains silent as if he's waiting for the punch line. "Well," she asks, "What do you think of that?"

Just then Sally interrupts them, "Come on you two love birds, everyone's in the living room. We're playing spin the bottle, and we need you right now!"

All the teenagers sit down on the floor in a big circle, alternating boys, and girls, with their legs crossed. Fanny Gold, one of the toilet-tissue triplets who hangs around with Betty Ann, has the first turn at spin the bottle. She doesn't seem disappointed when the bottle stops in front of Bill, the handsome boy from Julie's math study group. Everyone's eyes open wide as Bill plants a wet kiss on Fanny's big fat mouth. There's a massive reaction from the crowd. Eventually, the bottle is in Julie's hand, and as she spins it, she prays it stops in front of Larry. Come on, Larry, she happily thinks to herself. As the bottle slows down, she realizes it isn't even close to Larry. Instead, it comes to a full stop in front of Sally.

Sally hollers, "Redo. I call a redo for Julie."

Julie starts to breathe hard, and she sticks her tongue out slightly from the side of her mouth while she concentrates on her second spin. This time the bottle stops directly in front of Henry, one of the other boys from her math study group. Betty Ann sneers at Julie as Henry reaches across the circle of teenagers and takes Julie in his arms. The next thing Julie knows is she's being transported somewhere else, and she can no longer hear the voices cheering them on while Henry gives her an incredibly passionate kiss on her lips. Julie feels strange in a way she's never felt before. She doesn't want the kiss to end even though she dislikes Henry enormously and thought of him as a pompous ass. However, she had to admit, he was a hell of a good kisser. When she comes to her senses, she discovers that the kiss has upset Larry so much that he stands up quickly and accidentally knocks a drink into Betty Ann's toilet-paper stuffed cleavage; thus, rendering her ample sized breasts as flat as a pancake.

Betty Ann screeches at Larry, "You're such a klutz!" Then runs out of the room and into the bathroom where she locks herself in and refuses to come out.

Larry glances at Julie, and she can see he appears tormented. She isn't sure what upset him more; being yelled at by Betty Ann in front of everyone or watching Julie enjoy that stupid kiss from Henry.

Larry searches for his coat while Fanny Gold talks to Betty Ann through the locked bathroom door. From where Julie is sitting in the center of the living room floor, it sounds as if Betty Ann is crying and asking Fanny to find her coat because she wants to leave as well. Meanwhile, Julie realizes that the only reason Henry gave her that big, juicy kiss was to piss off Larry, and that it had nothing to do with his feelings for her whatsoever.

CHAPTER FOUR

The following year, at the high school's commencement, Mr. Swartz hands out the last diploma and returns to the middle of the podium. He bangs on the microphone to make sure it's on before making his final announcement of the ceremony. He coughs to clear his throat. "The last item in the program today is the Brooklyn College Scholarship Award. This year only one person had a high enough score to qualify for the award in math and science she is, and…" his voice quivers, "she, yes I said

she, is our very first female recipient." He hesitates to clear his throat again and looks down at his shoes, "Would, Miss Julie Levine please come up to the podium to receive her award?"

There is no applause because the scholarship has always gone to a boy. A susurrus passes through the crowd as everyone in the audience is astonished. Julie walks past the hushed students and onto the stage to collect her prize. She reaches the microphone by standing on her tiptoes and addresses the class with a simple," Thank you". Then she gives Mr. Swartz a firm handshake, takes hold of her coveted prize, and walks off the stage.

Rose, her baby sister, catches up to her. "You did it, you showed them. I want to be just like you, sis!"

There's a complicated physics equation on the blackboard in a crowed college lecture hall. All the students are males with one exception-Julie who is completing the math homework problem with a white piece of chalk for her classmates to see. Her eyes are on the math problem, and she is unaware of snarky remarks being made by the boys regarding her work. When she completes the equation, she places the piece of chalk down and turns to face the audience with a great big smile on her face because she feels confident that she answered it correctly.

The physics professor says. "Behold gentlemen, if even a girl can do this problem, so can you. Now get back to work!"

Her fellow classmates appear surprised and agitated with her success, as she takes her seat the boy next to her scowls.

The physics professor continues, "This is the equation for escape velocity. Learn it or your rockets will never liftoff."

Julie giggles while she thinks about what she's going to wear to the fraternity party Saturday night and if she has time to do laundry when she gets home.

The students are almost exclusively male who make up Brooklyn College's School of Engineering and they're not considered by most to be party animals, but they are still a good fit for Julie.

#

When she arrives at the frat party, the music is blaring fifties rock and roll. They're drinking beer, dancing, and some of the couples are making out. Julie and the young man who invited her are off in the corner arguing. Julie abruptly removes the pin from her sweater and hands it back to him. She walks across the room and grabs a beer out of the hand of Stanley, a fellow classmate and swigs it down.

Stanley protests, "Hey! What in the…"

Julie interrupts, "Give me a break, my boyfriend just broke up with me!" She guzzles down the remainder of his beer.

Her admission intrigues him, and he opens two more bottles and hands her one.

"Hi, I'm Stanley. What's your name?"

With anger in her voice she replies, "Julie and I'm majoring in engineering! Do you have a problem with that?"

"No and I thought you looked familiar."

Just then an Elvis song comes on. It turns her frowny face into a smile, and she answers back, "Good. Let's dance!"

He doesn't know what to make of Julie. Awkwardly he expresses, "Hey I think you're pretty keen. Do you want to be my girlfriend?"

"How about we just dance for now?"

The spring semester flies by them, and Julie can't think of a single thing she doesn't like about Stanley, plus he's smart, studious and conscientious, but best of all he proudly boasts about his girlfriend the engineer.

#

That summer Stanley borrows an old Woody station wagon from a friend, so they can go to a drive-in movie that's all the rage. The moon is full and the glass inside the wagon is steamed up. They must turn the volume all the way up on the mono speaker hanging from the driver's side window to compensate for the loudness of chirping from the crickets. On the big screen is a movie starring Charlton Heston and he's playing Moses. It's the scene right before he casts down the Ten Commandments, and the sinners fall into the deep crevice. This is when Julie decides it is time to tell Stanley the truth about her feelings and her new situation with college.

"Stanley, at the intermission we need to talk about something.

"Sure." His eyes move away from hers and back onto the movie screen. She cuddles up to him on the bench seat and thinks about what she's going to tell him.

When the intermission music begins to play, she confesses, "Stanley, I really like you and have never had feelings for anyone else like this."

Stanley appears startled and inquires, "Is there a but coming?"

She giggles, "There's no but." Then she proudly blurts out, "I was accepted to USC with a full scholarship!"

Stanley is stunned at first, "I'm so happy and proud of you."

"Phew, I was so worried I was almost too afraid to tell you."

"Stanley pulls her head towards his and replies, "This is really big news." He mimics Ed Sulivan's way of saying really big. "How did your Momma and Pop take it?"

She explains with some difficulty, "Momma cried and doesn't want me to leave, and Pop cried too, but I truly believe his were tears of joy." She hesitates and then asks him, "How about you, what are your thoughts on this?"

"Well for starters this confirms I have the smartest girlfriend in Brooklyn, so now all we have to do is figure out how we can make this all work."

"She grins, "Ok, here are my thoughts." She rubs her chin and then continues, "We move out to Los Angeles together, you find a job while I finish getting my engineering degree."

"Wow, like we live together and sleep together every night."

She smirks, "Yup and do you know the name of their football team?"

"Not a clue!"

"The Trojans!"

Stanley smiles, "This is beginning to sound too good to be true."

His reaction makes Julie feel a sense of relief. She reaches over and plants a kiss on his lips. He questions her while she is tugging on his clothes, "Are you sure about this?"

To which she confirms, "I think so, as long as you'll be extra careful."

Just then the movie, *Ten Commandments*, resumes and it's dark again in the car.

"I swear-scouts honor." He assures her.

"Ok, but you were never a boy scout."

"I'll sign up first thing tomorrow." Stanley envelopes Julie with a passionate kiss and she acquiesces to him.

#

The year is 1961.

Stanley Rudofsky wheels his pregnant wife, Julie, up to the emergency room doors at the UCLA Medical center, and politely waits for a group of nurses and doctors to exit through them first. Meanwhile, his hysterical wife impatiently hollers at him, "I want drugs!" Then she gives him a dirty look for standing still.

Moments later, a beautiful, blond nurse wearing long fake eyelashes helps Julie onto the examining table and then peeks between her legs. Julie can't get over how much the nurse resembled the actress, Angie Dickinson, and wonders for a second why someone so pretty is doing this sort of work. Then Julie has a lucid thought and realizes that this is exactly the sort of girl who will land a young doctor for her husband and that explains her perfect hair, makeup, and manicured nails.

Julie asks sweetly, "Are you here to give me drugs?"

"Sorry, darling, you're too far along. What's this, your second baby?" The nurse prepares a huge enema and hesitates with it dangling above Julie while she waits for her reply. Julie ignores her question. Meanwhile the nurse rolls her over and jabs the enema into her buttock.

Julie finally replies, "No, damn you, it's my third, and where did Stanley go?"

The nurse says snappily, "There's no reason to be impolite." She replaces the sheet over Julie and tries to make her feel more comfortable before she announces, "I'm going to get the doctor."

Julie begs her, "Please don't leave me!"

The nurse ignores Julie's plea and dashes out of the room. Stanley stands in the shadow of the doorway and reluctantly enters the room after the nurse departed.

Julie points her finger at him and says, "Stanley, I'm going to kill you."

He replies innocently, "What did I do?"

"Why did it take you so long to get me to the hospital?"

"Debbie wasn't home, and we needed somebody to watch the boys for us. What was I supposed to do with them? Lock them in the trunk of the car for Christ Sake, Julie!" Julie grins and he says, "Seriously, do you have any idea how hot it is out there?"

Julie complains, "Plan B, Stanley. Why is it you never have one?"

"It's Saturday, and no one was around. Can you give me a break for once?"

She doesn't miss a beat and continues to hammer him as the contractions get closer together. She grimaces, "Did you at least call Momma and tell her to come?"

"Yes, she's on her way, and it should only take her four days by train to get from New York to LA." Stanley strokes her hair.

Julie barks, "Stop touching me! That's how you got me this way."

Lovingly Stanley continues, "Maybe we'll finally have the little girl you've always wanted."

"Just shut up, Stanley, and go find the doctor. I'm ready to push.

CHAPTER FIVE

It's very early in the morning and Julie is already up even though she has the day off from work. Her new baby Sara hasn't settled into a schedule yet and seems to have her days and nights reversed. Julie and Stanley's house is a modest slab ranch that resembles the home exhibited during the 1959 Kitchen Debates that took place in Moscow. It was touted by then Vice-President Nixon as "The house of the future," replete with every modern-day convenience to make the American homemaker's day a living dream.

Julie lovingly holds four-day-old Sara in her arms while

she walks around trying to comfort the colicky newborn.

Julie's shortened maternity leave makes every moment they

have together feel even more precious. Everyone else in the

house is still asleep. Julie walks to the window because she

can hear a nasty sounding fight coming from across the

street, which interrupts the peaceful hush in her house. The

baby is finally asleep on Julie's shoulder and her curiosity

makes watching the fight too irresistible. She quietly peeks

through the dusty venetian blinds to watch the commotion.

It is an argument between her neighbors, Debbie, and Joe.

Debbie and Joe's house is an exact replica of Julie and

Stanley's house only it's painted pink instead of green.

Debbie just placed the last of several crates of empty beer

bottles in the back of her shiny, brand new, white Valiant

station wagon and closes the door. Julie watches as Joe

walks over to Debbie while shouting at her. Joe's blue

Chevelle convertible is next to Debbie's car in their driveway. The driver's door of the Chevelle is left open with the car running.

Joe hollers at Debbie, "What are you doing?"

Debbie says with a nervous grin on her face, "I'm returning all of the empty beer bottles from your poker game for the deposit money."

Joe lights a cigarette and then pops open the rear door to the station wagon. He takes a quick inventory of the bottles with his pointed index finger and then yells again at Debbie. "You mean to tell me that your precious time isn't worth a buck fifty?"

"I'm sorry Joe."

Her apology only pisses him off more, and he becomes enraged, "Stop rummaging through the garbage like an old bag lady. I didn't marry no bum, Debbie!"

"Joe, I says I'm sorry."

Joe points his finger in her face. "The word is said, you idiot, not says. Now get that crap out of your new car or else!"

Debbie is red in the face as she moves the first of the many crates to the curb. Just then Joe heatedly jumps in his car, "You've made me late for my meeting!" and squeals out of the driveway with the cigarette hanging out of his mouth. As soon as he's out of sight, Debbie moves the crate back into the rear of her station wagon, ties a kerchief around her hair, and puts on her sunglasses. She looks especially sexy, like a movie star trying not to be recognized. When Debbie slowly pulls out of her driveway, she notices Julie watching from between the blinds, so she stops her car, then pulls into Julie's driveway and rolls down her car window, then smiles at Julie, and waves hello. Julie goes to greet her still holding the sleeping baby in her arms.

Debbie whispers, "I've been meaning to come by. Has your mother arrived?"

Julie answers, "Tonight, thank goodness."

Debbie rests her elbow in the open window when she says, "I'll stop over later to give you a break from the boys, maybe take them to the park."

Julie is truly grateful for the offer. "Thanks, I could use the help. What was that all about between you and Joe?"

"Joe had another temper tantrum. He just hates it when I put anything dirty in the new car. If I told him I went to the dump, he'd have a heart attack."

Julie inquires, "Where are you going now?"

Debbie grins when she replies, "To the dump, then to the store to return a million empty beer bottles from Joe's poker game to get the bottle deposits back and to buy some hair color."

Julie seems puzzled. "Why? Your auburn hair's beautiful."

"Haven't you heard, blondes have more fun." Debbie fluffs up her hair from under the kerchief before she asks, "Want anything from the store?"

Julie thinks for a second before she answers, "No, but I'd love it if you took my empties too. I'd even be willing to pay you to help me clean out some of the crap in my garage."

The offer insults Debbie. "I could never take money from you. You're my friend."

Debbie gets out of her station wagon, glances at the adorable baby while she opens the trunk to her car, and comments, "She's a pretty little girl."

Julie sighs, "I know she is, and it almost makes me feel sorry for her." Julie hands the baby to Debbie and places four crates of empty bottles in the back of Debbie's station wagon. Then she reaches out to take back her sleeping baby and hesitates because she can see how much Debbie's enjoying holding her. After that Julie comments, "I guess that's all there's room for today and brushes her hands on her nightdress before she reaches for the baby. "Next time you go to the store, will you take some more of them for me and please at least keep that money?"

Debbie acquiesces to Julie's last request, "Okay, that's not unreasonable. Is there anything else I can do?"

Julie squeezes her hand, "No, but I want to thank you for helping me and for being my friend."

Debbie doesn't say another word, as she focuses on fitting some of the additional crates of empty bottles in the back seat of her car. She slams the door closed, hops in, then drives away, as she turns the corner, she waves to Julie and smiles.

#

Later, that same day after Debbie returns home, she reaches to the back of the closet and moves around a couple of boxes until she finds a small, old hat box. She takes it down, opens it, and flips over an out-of-style black velvet hat that she only wears to funerals, she reveals a thick wad

of cash. She pulls money from out of her back pocket and

adds it to the wad. She carefully places the box back in the

deepest, darkest corner of the closet. After that she picks up

the bottle of hair color and while reading the directions, she

enters the master bathroom.

CHAPTER SIX

Julie is exhausted from sleep deprivation, but still has one

eye open and can't doze off. Sara rests in her blue, worn

around the edges, hand-me-down basinet next to their bed.

Stanley and their Labrador Retriever Mousse, (as in the

pudding), are having trouble dealing with the many

interruptions during the night, as she's sprawled out at the

bottom of their bed and Stanley is snoring.

Julie hears Mathew call out from the bathroom, "Mommy, Daddy come quick! I pooped a chocolate ice cream in potty."

Stanley rises slowly and whispers, "You sleep! I'll go." Julie grunts and rolls over. The dog follows Stanley. Stanley returns with Matthew on his hip. "It's pretty awesome. It looks exactly like a soft serve chocolate ice cream centered perfectly in the bowl."

Julie reaches for Matthew and pulls him into the bed.

Stanley adds, "You've gotta go see this."

Julie reluctantly stands up as her body fights gravity. She looks in the potty but it's empty and she wonders if they're pulling her leg. Then she looks at her dog and it's licking its lips. She declares, "You didn't!" The dog looks guilty and runs out.

The next morning Julie's disheveled hair, dark circles around her eyes, and untied shoelaces are not the only indications of how overtired she is feeling. Otherwise, she's dressed and ready for work after her truncated maternity leave. She stands over her young sons and supervises their breakfast while she tries to eat something nourishing before rushing to the office. Maria, her housekeeper, is feeding Sara from a bottle, but the baby pushes it away as she cries for her mother's breast. Maria gazes up at Julie with a look of hopelessness in her eyes to express her frustration over her inability to feed the colicky newborn.

The TV in the living room is on, and it was viewable from the kitchen. Julie's two little boys transform into zombies while they watch a rerun episode of The Jetsons and munch on cornflakes. Jane Jetson is wearing a mask as she answers her space-age audiovisual telephone. The mask disguises how bad she looks in the morning with no makeup on and her hair in hair in curlers. When Jane Jetson sneezes and her mask blows off her face, the two boys laugh so hard that the younger one slams his hand on the table and knocks over his glass of orange juice.

Julie ignores the spill, as it splatters on the floor, and she glances at her watch. Her heart pounds in her chest. She begins to feel desperate for time and hollers down the hall to Stanley. She urges him to come and help with the kids, "What's taking you so long? Hurry up and get in here."

He replies from the bedroom while putting on his sneakers, "Just go already, we'll be fine."

Julie kisses each one of the kids, grabs her briefcase, and runs out the door.

#

She drives her two-tone '58 Chevy Bel Air station wagon with the window rolled down so she can rest her elbow and hold up her tired head. The wind on her face helps to revive her. When she reaches the security gate, she flashes her ID badge for the uniformed guard who opens it for her. She drives up to the business complex and completely ignores the ominously large sculpture of an Atlas rocket placed in front of the main building as if the sculpture wasn't there.

She enters the garage, and her heart begins to pound again while she searches for a space. She must drive up the seven levels to reach the roof until she finally finds a place to park.

When she arrives in her office, her desk is cluttered with a huge pile of unopened mail, interoffice memos, and unread reports marked urgent; they make her gasp as she turns on the desk lamp. She sits down immediately and attacks the stack with her letter opener. Jean, her secretary, enters, places a steaming cup of black coffee on Julie's desk, and exits without saying a word to her. Soon after, there is a knock at Julie's partially opened door to her tiny office: she looks up and sees Joshua, a handsome, single man in his late thirties who is always meticulously dressed. He is her closest friend at work and confidant, but also there's something about him that makes him unthreatening to Stanley, which she appreciates. He gives her a peck on the cheek, the kiss is awkward because he's holding a baby gift that's wrapped in pink paper with lots of ribbons and bows. He struggles not to drop it when he leans over her desk.

Julie exclaims, "Wow, it's wrapped so pretty I don't think I'm ever going to open it."

"Open it!" He pleads. "It's been taking up space in my office for over a week."

Julie enthusiastically rips it open. Inside is a gorgeous tiny yellow dress with hand-stitched smocking. Next to it are pairs of matching shoes and lace-frilled socks. "Sara will look incredible in this!" Then she looks up and asks with a worried tone in her voice, "Was I missed?"

"Missed? When Kennedy heard you were out on another maternity leave, he called Khrushchev to request a halt to the space race until you returned."

Julie smiles as she replies, "I missed you too. Any good gossip while I was gone?"

"Yes, there's tons of it. Susie from the typing pool is having an affair with Fred from engineering."

"He's such a pig," she says with a giggle.

Joshua adds, "A married pig with kids, but the big news is that the Russians decided they want another milestone for the history books."

She is genuinely worried. "Oh no, what is it this time?"

"They're about to launch a cosmonaut named Valentina, so now they'll have not only the first man in space, but also the first woman."

"Do you think we'll ever train a woman to be an astronaut?"

His answer is short and to the point, "Nope."

"Is there any good news?"

He claps his hands together, "Best for last, NASA is giving our project the green light."

"No way! I can't believe we won the contract for the lunar excursion module." They dance up and down and hug each other.

Joshua continues, "Oh, and one more thing. Phil wants a word with you."

"Shit! How do I look?" she asks.

"Truthfully, you look dreadful." He makes this remark as if it were a matter of fact.

"All right, I'll freshen up before I see him."

Joshua agrees, "That will be time well spent."

Julie stands up and says, "Wish me luck!"

#

Julie forgets to take her jacket with the ID badge attached to it when she dashes off to meet up with Phil. Her first stop on the way is the ladies' room to express her aching breasts. After she flushes the toilet and leaves the stall, she bumps into someone she has never met before. They look one another up and down while the stranger leans close to the mirror making up her already overly made-up face. She greets Julie with a smile. "Hi doll." She pops her gum and continues to tease her hair.

Julie is curious. "Are you new here?"

The woman looks directly at Julie as she says, "I was wondering the same thing about you."

"I've been here since '58." Julie replies.

"Wow, I started in '60. How is it we've never met?"

Julie tries to fix her makeup with the few dried-out old items in her handbag, but she is not very good at it. The woman steps in without an invitation and takes over.

"Looks like you could use some help."

Julie accepts, and the woman pulls a large makeup bag out from her oversized, fake snakeskin handbag. She starts by fixing Julie's eyebrows, then she dabs some foundation on her face and says, "My complexion is much darker than yours, so it's going to make you look like you have a tan."

Julie laughs out loud, "Today's my first day back after a leave of absence. They'll think I was sitting with my feet up, drinking margaritas in Acapulco."

Then she paints Julie's full lips with pink frosted lipstick, puts some thick black eyeliner on her upper eyelids, and adds a little bit of frosted eye shadow to make her look more awake. When she finishes, she steps back to look at Julie and comments, "Not bad."

Julie looks into the mirror and says, "I don't recognize myself!"

The woman hands Julie the makeup she used on her face and motions with her hands, "Please keep it. By the way, how come you're not wearing an ID badge?"

Julie reaches for it and realizes she had left it behind, "Oh no, it's clipped to my jacket back in my office." She stretches out her arm, and reaches to shake the woman's hand in gratitude, and says, "Hi, I'm Julie."

"I'm Penny." Right after she introduces herself, her curiosity grows because Julie mentioned she has an office. "Which engineer are you assigned to?"

Julie grins as she replies, "Levine-Rudofsky."

Penny adds another coat of lipstick before she asks, "Does this Levine or Rudofsky give you a hard time?" Penny winks at Julie in the mirror. "If you know what I mean."

"No. Why, does your boss?"

"That fat hog tries to get a piece of this every single disgusting day!" Sneers Penny as she twists around and pinches her own rump.

Julie innocently asks, "Why don't you tell him to cut it out?"

"Oh yeah, he'll just apologize to me and promise to never do it again. Wake up! I need the job, and he knows it."

Julie defends herself, "I need my job, too, but I wouldn't take that kind of crap."

Penny whines, "It's my reality. I'm divorced with two kids. My ex skipped out on us, and the only things he left me were unpaid bills, and a cold sore."

"I feel so sorry for you."

Penny complains, "What is it with me? I must give off the stench of desperation or something." Penny sprays her hair when she uses the word stench.

"Penny, have you ever heard anything about Levine-Rudofsky in engineering?"

Penny mulls the question over in her mind for a moment, "No, not even heard the names before.

Why, are those guys assholes too?"

"I hope not, and also it's she."

"Now I know you're pulling my leg."

Julie responds with pride in her voice, "No I'm not, and I am Julie Levine-Rudofsky."

Penny stops fixing her hair, then turns toward Julie when she questions her, "No way! You're a girl rocket scientist?"

Julie boasts, "I prefer to think of myself as a woman aerospace engineer."

"Oh, my goodness, will you allow me to worship the ground you launch from?"

Julie isn't sure if Penny's comment was sincere or sarcastic.

"That's really not necessary."

But Penny is intrigued and continues, "How the hell did you sneak past all of those bastards?"

"I've been lucky, I guess. They somehow forgot what I am and accepted me as a man with a vagina."

"Julie, I'm the fastest and most accurate typist in the pool. If you're ever in a jam, and I mean ever, you can count on me."

"Thanks, Penny, and I've got your back also."

CHAPTER SEVEN

When Julie arrives at Phil's office, his secretary, Florence, quickly ends what appears to be a personal telephone call and smiles at Julie. "How's the new baby?" She claps her hands together in anticipation of the details.

Julie beams while she replies, "Sara is a delight. I can already tell that raising a daughter is quite different from my experience with her brothers. Stanley will be picking up her pictures at the drug store on his way home tonight."

Florence admits, "I wouldn't know. I've only the one son, and he's already in high school. I'm so envious of you, Julie. I've always wanted a little girl. I believe there's something magical between a mother and a daughter."

"Florence, please feel free to come over for a visit. So how have you been?"

"Just great! My son made first string quarterback on the varsity team. We're so proud of him. Let me tell Phil you're here."

Florence pushes a button on her intercom and announces, "Julie's here to see you, Phil."

Phil is sitting at his desk smoking a cigarette and drinking coffee when Julie enters his office. She sits down across from him. He looks at her dolled-up face and makes a lupine smile. "Julie, you look wonderful, and I'm not just saying it."

"Thanks." She replies while she squirms in Phil's uncomfortable, ultramodern, space age chair. She is still tender from giving birth to Sara and doesn't appreciate the feeling of the hard, molded plastic seat beneath her.

Phil continues, "You were sorely missed from your department, and I'm glad you came back to us so soon. I truly believe your contribution was an integral part in our winning the bid at NASA."

"Thanks again, Phil."

Phil offers her a cigarette, and she motions no thanks. "There was some talk while you were gone, 'What if she leaves us to take care of her family?' Want to know what I said to that?"

She placates him. "Sure, Phil."

"Well, I told them you already manage a big family, and you're not going anywhere, you're just like one of the guys."

She replies with relief, "Thanks for standing up for me while I was on maternity leave. There's something I want to ask you."

"Shoot. You know I'd do anything for you, kid."

Julie understands exactly how to manipulate Phil. She leans in toward him as if she were about to tell him a secret and reveals, "Roberts has been trying to steal Jean from me, and now that I'm back, I'm going to let him have her." Then she sits back in the chair and waits for Phil to solve her problem for her.

"Wow, that's awfully nice of you. Do you have any preference for a replacement?"

"My first choice is Penny from the typing pool."

Phil brags, "Consider it done. I'll let Roberts know the good news, and I'll personally remind him that he owes you one."

Julie is anxious and stands up for her next request. Phil appears confused by this. Julie takes a deep breath and blurts quickly before she loses her nerve, "I've got one more thing to ask you."

Phil motions for her to continue. "Anything babe, you know you're my go-to girl."

Julie looks up at the ceiling as if she is awaiting divine intervention before plunging in. "While I was on maternity leave, I visited the technical institute that's nearby."

Phil is startled, "Why the hell did you go there?"

"To apply to their graduate school," she confesses.

"What happened?"

She's embarrassed, "They turned me down, and told me the school doesn't admit girls."

Phil sighs and slowly folds his hands, "How can I help?"

"Phil, please get me into the company's tuition reimbursement program. I haven't given up my dream to get my master's degree in engineering."

He's surprised that she would pick such a busy time in her life to pursue something like this. "Are you sure you're up to it with all the other things you have going?"

"Yes, I am," she states confidently.

Phil lets out another sigh, looks at Julie, and pushes down the intercom button. "Florence, please bring me the forms for the tuition reimbursement program."

"By the way, I came here today because you wanted to see me.

Phil reaches into his top desk drawer. "Oh, thanks for reminding me. I have a gift for the new baby." He hands her a small, wrapped package. "Congratulations."

On the way back to her office Julie walks by the typing pool. There are four rows with three desks in each with a large state of the art electric typewriter on top. All the typists are Caucasian woman with bleach blond hair, except for Penny who stands out like a sore thumb. They're similarly dressed and working in unison like robots. There is something musical about the rhythm of their work, and their faces are devoid of expression. Just at that moment, Penny pulls from her typewriter a completed page. She looks up to give her stiff neck a brief rest and makes eye

contact with Julie. She silently mouths, "Get me out of

here, please!"

CHAPTER EIGHT

FALL 1963

Julie is sitting on top of her unmade queen-sized bed and studying for her master's degree. She is sharing her space with a pile of stuffed animals, the family's dog, and a variety of storybooks. Her three young children, David, Matthew, and Sara are playing in the living room. Their noise level is climbing and becoming a constant distraction.

Julie can hear *My Favorite Martian* playing in the background, and from the shrieks she surmises no one is watching TV. Stanley is practicing his clarinet for an upcoming event at the local college where he teaches engineering. He is going over the same piece of music, making her feel as if she's going crazy. Although he is thoughtful and went to the garage to work on his runs, she can still hear him through the uninsulated walls of the house. What Julie doesn't know is that Debbie is with the children and she's the instigator. It's her antics that are the main reason they're behaving so wildly and out of control.

Debbie cackles just like the Wicked Witch of the West and says, "I'm going to get you, my pretties." The kids run around the sofa with Debbie chasing after them. The family's golden retriever joins in the fun by playfully barking at the kids. Debbie is glistening with sweat when the dog jumps over the sofa to catch David and pin him down, then the dog runs past the coffee table and knocks over Debbie's full can of Tab. The dog immediately stops chasing the children and begins to lap up the Tab on the coffee table.

Julie decides to take a break from studying and goes to the living room to find out what's causing the mayhem. The room is a complete mess, and she isn't happy about the spilled soda that's dripping off the coffee table and onto the beige carpet. That is also when Julie realizes she has a houseguest. She takes a long look at Debbie and sighs when she realizes who the ringleader is. Julie still can't get over how different Debbie looks. She had transformed her hair from a flattering auburn color to a shockingly light shade of blonde.

Julie hollers, "Time out!"

The children ignore her and continue to run around the living room. That is the reason why when a special announcement about President Kennedy runs across the bottom of the television screen it goes unnoticed. Instead,

Julie turns the TV off and tries to grab Sara, who giggles wildly as she moves past her mother.

Julie yells louder this time. "Stop running in the house!"

Debbie looks up at Julie as if she notices her for the first time since she entered the living room.

When Julie has the children's attention, she demands, "All three of you, march into the bathroom and wash your hands right now and then sit down at the kitchen table for lunch." They obediently follow her directions.

Julie turns to Debbie and asks, "What has gotten into you?"

Debbie confesses, "It's the event at the club next month. It's making me so nervous."

Julie makes the sandwiches for the kids, then turns toward Debbie and inquires, "Why's that?"

"It's a dinner dance for the holidays," she replies.

Julie is confused. "I don't follow you."

Debbie continues, "We'll be sitting at Joe's boss's table,

and Joe asked me to wear something nice."

"I still don't get it."

Debbie goes on to explain, "I'm making this green silk dress that I saw in *Red Book*. So, I bought the pattern."

They both sit at the kitchen table with the kids, and Debbie shows Julie the torn-out page from the magazine with a picture of a skintight dress.

Julie asks, "What does that have to do with you acting so crazy?"

"Oh, I'm sorry about that. I took a diet pill to help me get into the dress."

Her reason confuses Julie even more, so she replies, "I thought you were sewing it. Why not make it to fit you?"

Debbie smiles. "I want it to go on tight, that's why!"

"This sounds nuts to me. Do you want to have some lunch with us?"

"I'll stay, but all I want is Metrical, and I know where you keep them." Debbie stands up from the kitchen table and goes to the fridge. She grabs a cold can of strawberry-flavored Metrical and pops open the lid. She turns around to ask, "Do you have a straw?"

Julie bites into her peanut butter and jelly sandwich and has a full mouth of food. She points toward the cupboard near the sink.

Julie pours milk into jelly jars for the kids while Debbie is sipping her Metrical from a straw. David isn't satisfied with his regular flavored milk and goes to get the Ovaltine. Julie likes the idea of chocolate milk and mixes it into their four jelly jars of milk. She must push over a stack of mail to make room for the jar of Ovaltine on the crowded table. Then she takes another big bite of her sandwich and savors the sweet taste in her mouth. The AM transistor radio is on in the background, but no one was listening to it.

"So, why didn't you go to work today?" asks Debbie.

"Maria wanted a day off, and Stanley's rehearsing for a musical event at the college tonight."

Debbie appears hurt. "Why didn't you ask me to help you out? You know how much I love to spend time with your kids."

Julie washes down a mouthful of her peanut butter and jelly sandwich with chocolate milk. "I didn't want to impose on you, that's why."

Julie's and Debbie's heads both turn at the same time toward the AM radio when they hear the song on the radio end in the middle, as it was interrupted by a special announcement. "President Kennedy was shot today in Dallas, Texas. Vice President Johnson has taken the oath of office. The doctors have reported that the President is dead."

Julie drops the remainder of her sandwich, runs out of the kitchen, and goes to the living room. She turns on the TV and flips through the channels on the dial until she locates Walter Cronkite on CBS. Julie is mesmerized and forces herself to look up from TV. She hollers, "David, go get Daddy!"

Julie reaches for the telephone and cradles the receiver under her chin while she dials. Her voice is shaky, and she says, "It's me, Julie. Please, put Joshua on the phone."

She taps her foot while she waits for him to pick up. "Joshua, what's going on over there?" She listens intently to his answer and asks, "How are you holding up?"

After he explains how he is feeling, she says, "You shouldn't be alone at a time like this. Come straight to my house after work."

She looks up and realizes that Stanley is in the room, and he doesn't know why she sent for him. He is holding his clarinet while waiting patiently for her to get off the telephone.

Julie says into the telephone, "We'll see you later." Then she hangs up and turns to Stanley.

He appears worried. "Julie, David said that you needed me."

"Come watch the news. It's just terrible!" Julie is in shock from it, she can't find the words to tell Stanley.

Stanley sits next to her; she holds Sara in her lap and tenderly strokes the soft ringlets in her hair while she tries to hold back her tears. Debbie joins them on the sofa just as the two boys dash out the front door because they hear the musical jingle of the bells coming from the ice cream truck up the street.

CHAPTER NINE

It is 7 a.m. when Julie arrives at work. Even though it's
early she still must run to get to the special meeting in the
cafeteria. It is already full, and there isn't an empty chair
anywhere in view. Joshua sees her and waves to get her
attention. He had saved an extra seat at his table for her, as
he predicted she might be the last to arrive. Already at the
table with him is Penny and Joshua's secretary, Linda. The
rest of the room is jammed with nervous aerospace

engineers waiting to hear about the fate of the company. With the death of President Kennedy, the big concern is that the space race might be over, which would mean the end of their jobs as well.

Phil adjusts the height of the microphone and looks around. The people seated are almost exclusively young white men. There are a handful of women, but they are mostly secretaries or switchboard operators, and the only people of color appear to be from ground maintenance and building management and they are mainly standing on the perimeter of the room. Phil waits for the stragglers to arrive before he begins.

Joshua barely notices anything going on around him in the cafeteria. He's wearing his tortoise shell Ray Bans like a mask to hide his bloodshot eyes, which were swollen from crying over the death of John F. Kennedy and the half a pint of whiskey he found in his glovebox and drank to get himself to sleep at 3am. It has affected everyone hard, but

Joshua seems to be more sensitive about this tragedy than the rest of the men at work.

Phil accidentally coughs into the microphone, and when he looks up at the crowd, he realizes that he has everyone's undivided attention. He is nervous and begins to perspire, as he is not fond of speaking to large crowds. His face and large forehead are glistening when he says, "Good morning, everyone, and thank you for coming in to work so early today." He coughs again while he attempts to clear the tightness in his throat, and then he continues while trying to suppress his emotions. "President Johnson sent out a directive to remind us of what our job is, and it is my duty as your boss to share it with you. In honor of President Kennedy's memory, the United States of America will put the first man on the moon and do so in this decade."

Phil's eyes fill with tears as he folds the paper he read and puts it in his shirt pocket. He has a stern expression as he scans the audience. He continues, "When you go back to your offices today, remember one thing and one thing only.

Nothing else matters until we…" Phil points to the people

in the room, "Put the first man on the moon. Now all of you

get to back to work!"

Phil wipes the sweat from his forehead with his

handkerchief and walks away from the microphone. Julie,

Joshua, and Penny sit together while they wait for the

others to exit. At another table nearby is a group of young

secretaries, and Julie thinks she recognizes one of the

women from her past. She resembles one of her nemeses

from high school, Fanny Gold. Fanny is unaware Julie is

watching her, as she continues talking to her co-workers.

#

Julie must remain at work until late that night to solve a

serious problem with an upcoming satellite launch. Her

career depends on her success and this sudden tragedy is

badly distracting her team. She had been there since the 7

a.m. meeting, so it was an especially long day. She is tired, hungry, and thirsty. When she rises from her desk and reaches for the empty decanter the offices are dark, so Julie believes everyone has left. She is filling the decanter at the bubbler when she hears some strange noises. She walks toward where they're coming from and hesitates in front of an office door.

Julie stares at the nameplate on the closed door and then notices a slit of light coming from under it. She is holding a paper cup of water in one hand and her decanter in the other. She stands outside the door and listens for a moment. It is plainly obvious to her that the people inside that office are fornicating. She looks again at the nameplate and in disgust mutters under her breath, "Fred, you're such a pig." She finishes her water, tosses the paper cup in the wastebasket, and turns around to go back to her office.

Julie sits at her desk and goes right back to work on her satellite problem. Just then her telephone rings; it makes her jump, and she accidentally knocks over her second cup of water. It runs all over her paperwork. As she answers the phone, she reaches for tissues to soak up the mess.

The man on the telephone introduces himself as a police officer and Julie can hear Sara crying in the background. "Hi, are you Sara's mother?"

"Yes, I am."

While continuing to calm Sara the police officer says, "See I told you, Sara. Your mommy is not on her way to the moon." Then he speaks clearly to Julie, "I've got your little girl here at the police station. It appears no one came to pick her up after Ballet, so she tried walking home on her own and one of officers saw her wandering the street and brought her to me."

"I'm on my way! What's your address?" She writes it down, grabs her purse, and the wet paperwork. "Thank you, officer." She hangs up the telephone, turns off her desk light, shuts her door and dashes toward the elevator.

She doesn't hesitate to think why the elevator door is

already open and walks straight into Susie and Fred who are in the middle of a passionate embrace. They are so engrossed they don't notice her at first. Julie remains silent as they descend in the shaft, but by the time the elevator reaches the lobby Susie and Fred turn as red as a ripe tomato from embarrassment. Julie says nothing to them, not even goodnight. She rushes straight to her car, and she can feel her heart pounding in her chest. She is so anxious and upset she drops her car keys twice before opening the car door that she forgot to lock in the first place. All that is on her mind is getting to her little girl and calming her down.

It's late when Julie and Sara walk in the kitchen. Stanley is practicing his clarinet in the living room like nothing is wrong when Julie angrily throws down her briefcase and purse, along with her water-stained satellite notes which flutter to the floor. David and Matthew are at the table eating the remains of their TV dinners and drinking Tang.

Julie hollers, "Stanley!"

The music suddenly stops. Stanley strolls in and goes to kiss her. She pushes him away and gives him the death stare.

He's petrified, "What's the matter?"

Julie says in a raised voice, "Do you know where I've been, Stanley?

"No."

"At a police station picking up our daughter."

He's horrified, "I thought she went home with Becky after ballet. I must have mixed up my days."

Sara cries hysterically, "Becky was out sick today!" The boys are frightened and stop eating."

Julie loses it and starts yelling, "Stanley, the satellite launch is in less than a week. I didn't need this from you tonight!" Julie slams her hand down hard on the counter next to the huge pile of unpaid bills.

Stanley looks at the pile and pleads with her, "I'll take

care of those first thing."

Julie lowers her voice, "Matthew, are you prepared for your math test tomorrow?"

"Ugh, I think so."

She gives him a stern look, "I haven't seen you study once this week. Go to your room now and do your homework!" He starts to cry as he gets up.

Then she turns to look David in the eyes, "Did you tell Sara that I went to the moon?"

David snickers at the question and nods yes to her. "David, go to your room right now!"

Stanley begs her, "I'm sorry, Julie."

She confesses to Stanley, "I can't do this anymore!"

CHAPTER TEN

Penny enters Julie's office and says enthusiastically, "Hey someone from Look Magazine is on the phone and wants to talk to you.

Julie mutters under her breath, "I bet Stanley didn't pay the bill for our subscription.

Penny giggles, "No, silly. They want to photograph you standing next to the scale model of the satellite in the lobby." Julie hesitates with her hand on the telephone sitting in its cradle.

Penny eagerly points to the telephone. "Pick up the phone! They're downstairs and want you join them right now!"

Julie brushes her hair back with her hand and say sarcastically, "Sure, like this is a good time." Julie presses the flashing button on her phone and says, "Hello, sure I'll be right down."

A professional photographer snaps shots of Julie standing next to the Satellite and for the first time in her life Julie feels recognized for her contribution to the project.

In the control room late at night Julie watches with her fellow engineers and project managers as the countdown moves closer to blast off. During the last ten seconds she holds her breath. In a flash the rocket explodes upon liftoff, and everyone gasps from the shock.

Julie pinches herself between her eyes and shakes her

head in disbelief.

The following morning Julie is back at her desk. All sorts of concerns rush through her thoughts. She wonders who is going to be blamed, who will get the ax and who might get promoted because of the new opening. These thoughts give her a shiver. She presses her intercom button, "Penny, are you busy?"

Penny replies over the intercom, "Frightfully, why?"

"Can you come in anyway? I need you right away."

Penny enters and sits down across from Julie. Penny is holding a pencil and pad to take shorthand notes. Penny asks anxiously, "Am I in any trouble? Phil's speech is still giving me the willies and with the satellite disaster I'm wondering if I need to be looking for a job."

Julie looks into Penny's eyes. "No, and don't worry about leaving early to take your son to the doctor; I've got it covered for you."

"Praise Jesus, my prayers have been answered."

"How's that exactly?" Julie asks her.

"The last time I went to church, I asked the lord to send me the love of my life."

Julie asks naively, "So, you've met someone new?"

"No, silly, the lord sent you to me."

Julie shuffles some of the papers on her desk. "I love you too, Penny, but let's get to work. Now that things have quieted down, I want you to go down to personnel and find out what you can about a woman named Fanny Gold.

"Might I ask why?"

Julie is in a rush and answers, "I'll tell you later. I'm late for a meeting." Julie dashes out of her office and leaves Penny with her mouth open, as if she were about to ask another question.

Julie runs to Joshua's office and glances at her watch on the way. She couldn't believe how long she had kept him waiting. Joshua is looking over plans when Julie burst into his cluttered office. There are variations of scaled models of the Command Service Module on the floor and shelves filled with piles of space-age fabric, samples, and swatches.

Julie apologizes, "I'm sorry I made you wait."

Joshua greets her nonchalantly and says, "I kept myself busy."

Julie closes the door to his office behind her. Joshua's secretary, Linda, looks at them curiously through the crack in the door as it closes.

Joshua boasts, "People are going to think there's something going on between us."

Julie grins when she replies, "You're the best-looking man here. I should be so lucky."

Joshua becomes suddenly suspicious, "You're awfully complimentary this morning. You must want a favor or some help. Which is it?"

"Both." Julie looks down while she waits for his reply.

Joshua taps his right index finger against his lips and thinks about her dilemma for a moment, "Let me guess, you're pregnant again."

Julie rebukes, "Bite your tongue."

Joshua is frustrated when he asks her, "So, what can I do for you today?"

Julie explains, "We've received an RFP from the Lunar Excursion Module's contractor."

Joshua attempts to complete her sentence, "And I'm guessing you've some bright ideas about how to build it?"

Julie admits proudly, "Yes I do, but getting Phil to listen to me is another story."

Joshua sounds genuinely confused, "I don't know why you feel that way."

Julie stands up and walks over to the window. "It's simple; they're never going to pick a woman to design it."

Joshua complains, "Stop feeling sorry about being a woman. Things are starting to change; just think about the fact there's never been a man on the moon before either."

"True, so does this mean I can count on you for your

support?"

The urgent tone in her voice worries him. "Julie, this could blow up in your face like the satellite just did, and we could both end up without a job."

"You know dam well that wasn't my fault. It blew up on the launch pad because the technicians weren't careful while monitoring the barometric pressure."

"It was still your project and that makes the Max Q part of your wheelhouse of problems as well, and you sure as hell blew that to bits."

She states begrudgingly, "Joshua, I know that I'm asking a lot, but I can't do this without you."

Joshua runs his fingers through his hair while trying to decide what to tell her. "I need to think about it, and I'll get back to you with my answer."

"Will you let me know soon?"

Joshua reluctantly states, "Yes and soon."

His response disappoints her. She nervously smooths

her damp palms over the creases in her skirt, and abruptly

leaves his office without saying goodbye.

CHAPTER ELEVEN

Julie and Stanley are in bed. Stanley is watching *Lost in Space* on TV and Julie is engrossed in the book, *The Feminine Mystique*. Sara and Matthew are asleep between Stanley and Julie leaving no room for the dog; he has nowhere left to go except the floor. At the TV commercial for Breck shampoo, Stanley turns to Julie and taps her gently.

"What are you reading?"

She answers, "A book my sister sent me."

"Is it any good?"

"It's informative," she mumbles.

Stanley looks down at his folded hands and hesitates before he asks his next question, "I hate to bring this up, but are we ever going to do "it" again?"

Julie raises her voice when she explains, "Stanley, you know how fertile I am!"

He says with a sulk, "So?"

She groans, "I'm working towards a promotion, and they're not going to give it to a woman with a big belly."

Stanley appeals to her, "I'll be extra careful."

"That's what you said right before I conceived Sara, David, and Matthew."

Stanley's head slumps, "So, I should take that as a no."

Just then the telephone rings, and Julie grabs it right away so not to wake everyone up. The kids and dog are undisturbed, and Stanley returns to watching the TV show. Julie places her book on the night table and takes the call.

"Hello?" She listens for a moment. "No, you're not disturbing me, Joshua."

While Julie listens, she notices a hole in one of Stanley's grungy, old socks. She focuses on his exposed jagged, dirty toenail; from her facial expression it is clear she is beginning to find him repulsive.

When Joshua stops talking, she replies, "You mean it? Wow, thank you so much. I promise you; I'm not going to let you down."

#

The next morning, Julie enters her stuffy, windowless office and throws her purse down on her desk in disgust. She looks at her tiny space and gasps. It's inconceivable to her that she's working at a higher level than Joshua, has completed her master's degree, and is still in an office not much bigger than a broom closet. She decides at that moment that she is going to get what she deserves. A window to look out of to help her focus and a much bigger office.

After she collects her thoughts, she calls Penny and asks her to come in, so they can go over a few things. Penny enters while bragging about what a great job she did collecting the information about Fanny Gold, "That was no easy task, I tell you."

Julie asks, "Why's that?"

"First of all, they wanted to know why I needed this information."

It hadn't occurred to Julie they would question Penny. "So, what did you tell them?"

"Since I had no clue why I was snooping around, I panicked."

This information upsets Julie. "Oh, my goodness, what did you say?"

"I said that Fred is in need of another secretary for his

department, so he wanted some background information on Fanny."

Penny's answer is a relief to Julie. "That was quick thinking. What did you find out?"

"At first there was nothing, as there was no Fanny Gold. But while everyone was at lunch, I went through the files one by one until I found a Fanny Stone from Brooklyn, New York."

"Wow, I'm impressed." Julie sits back in her chair and takes a sip of her coffee while she listens to the rest.

"At the very least I owed you the time from the other day."

Julie's mind drifts away for a moment while she digests Penny's report. Then she comments, "Stone, nobody's named Stone back where I come from. Her husband must have changed it from something else, like Stein."

"What are you talking about, that's a very common name."

Julie grins and says, "Maybe in Texas, but my people back in Brooklyn are Silvermans, Grossmans, and Cohens. There just aren't that many Stones!"

Penny reads from her stenography pad, "She's give or take a year or two older than you, she never went to college, like me, and she's married to an Air Force pilot. From what I could tell from her résumé, they don't have any children yet, and she started in the typing pool about three months ago." She snickers, "Lucky girl got my old job."

"Thanks, Penny."

Penny looks at Julie with wide-open eyes and is half sitting out of her chair. "Now it's your turn to tell me what this is all about."

"Fanny went to high school with me in Brooklyn. She and her two cohorts back in the day hated my guts because I'm smart, and they tried their hardest to make my life miserable."

"I guess it's payback time, isn't it?"

Julie sits straight up in her chair and reveals, "I've more important things to do, Penny."

Penny chuckles before she adds, "Plus, you're too classy."

"Thanks, again. Now let's put this behind us and focus on getting our work done."

CHAPTER TWELVE

Debbie enters the kitchen wearing no makeup, a pink terry cloth robe, fluffy matching slippers, and her hair is pinned up in soft foam clip-on curlers. The first thing she does is plug in the percolator. Then she looks around in the messy kitchen to survey the damage, and she smiles. There are empty beer bottles on the table, floor, countertop, and in the sink. The pink and grey Formica table is sticky and disgusting. There are four overflowing ashtrays, half-eaten deli sandwiches with crushed cigarettes poking out of them, greasy napkins, flakes of potato chips, piles of poker chips, and a deck of cards strewn on top of everything, as if the last player had thrown them down in disgust when he found out he lost his hand.

#

While Debbie is cleaning her kitchen, Julie is preparing her children for school. Julie waves goodbye as the bus picks them up. It's Sara's first day and the first time the house has been truly quiet in many years. When the bus moves away, it reveals Debbie as she loads several crates of empty bottles into the back of her station wagon. Her hair is still in the soft pink foam rollers, but she had changed into shorts and a matching blouse. Debbie waves to Julie as she drives off to do her errands. She starts to pull the rollers from her hair one by one as she goes around the corner.

Debbie drives to the center of town, parks her car, and walks into a small bank. She goes over to the bank's manager and politely asks him a question. "Excuse me, can you tell me how much it costs to rent a safety deposit box?"

"Do you mean a safe deposit box?" Then he prudently explains, "They come in three sizes. The smallest is $5 a year, up to our biggest box for $8. Would you like to see them?"

They cost more than she anticipated, so she feels embarrassed when she replies, "No, thank you."

Later that morning, Debbie decides to buy herself a treat. She sits on the park bench in the center of town across the street from the bank and enjoys a vanilla soft-serve ice cream cone that had been dipped in a strawberry hard-shell. She licks it quickly because it is a hot day, and the ice cream is melting down her wrist. After making a mess of herself, she goes straight home to clean up.

Debbie gets out of the car and casually walks to the front door of her house. Something is stuck in the mail slot, and she's curious as to what it is, so as she approaches her door, she sees it doesn't have an address written anywhere on its brown paper wrapping. She begins to untie the string while she opens the door, but she needs scissors to cut it. Debbie looks at it while she wonders where it came from. After she partially rips it open, she discovers a short note tucked inside. She reads it aloud: "Debbie, my sister gave this book to me, and now I'm passing it along to you. Love, Julie." Debbie peels off more of the brown paper and reveals the book's title, *The Feminine Mystique*.

After Debbie enters the house, she drops her keys into the bowl on the table near the front door, kicks off her shoes, makes herself comfortable on the sofa, breaks open the string, and begins to read the book.

That night she makes an elaborate dinner for Joe. The table is set with their fine China and lighted candles. She pours his favorite red wine to go along with the meal and tosses a big Caesar salad. Afterward, she toasts fresh garlic bread with a parsley garnish. Joe saunters into the kitchen while removing his tie. He has gained a bit more weight, and his clothes are too tight. When he removes his hat, his receded hairline makes him look older than his actual age.

Joe says in praise of her efforts, "Yum, something sure smells good. What's for dinner?"

"Italian," she replies with emphasis on the "I"."

"Great! I'm famished." Joe puts a couple of ice cubes in a crystal glass and pours himself a double shot of scotch. Then he lights a cigarette and takes a gulp of his drink. He makes eye contact with Debbie, and she smiles at him while on her way to the dinner table with the salad. Joe and Debbie sit across from each other. She places the remainder of the food with the plated salad on the table in front of them.

Joe comments, "Everything looks wonderful. You must have slaved over it all day."

Debbie blushes from the compliment and then asks him, "Garlic bread?"

He nods and she passes the basket to him and adds.

"Grated Parmesan cheese?"

Joe gratefully accepts, "Thanks, yes, please."

Debbie gets up to give Joe the grated cheese, and then she places spaghetti on his plate for him and sits down to serve herself. While Joe is twirling the spaghetti on his fork Debbie speaks up, "Hypothetically, if you had some extra money, what would you do with it?"

Debbie's question surprises Joe, and he answers her with a mouthful of food. "Since when do you use words like hypothetically?"

"Joe, you're not married to an empty chair. I read plenty, so answer my question."

Joe thinks about it for a moment before he answers her. "Well, I'd find a stockbroker with a good track record and invest the money wisely." Joe looks over at Debbie and gives her a scrutinizing look. "Debbie, are you worried about our retirement, or if something happens to me?"

Debbie's mouth was full of spaghetti, and she shrugs

maybe.

The idea that she is worried about him providing for her upsets him and he wonders why she's digging into their finances. "Baby, I make plenty of dough, and I've been socking it away for a while."

Joe lights another cigarette and takes a big swig of the red wine. Then he stuffs more bread in his mouth. He speaks while holding a big chunk of bread in his hand and while chewing a mouthful of food. "First thing tomorrow, I'll look into a life insurance policy that will take care of you if anything happens to me."

Debbie is relieved that Joe has no clue what she was asking him about and says sweetly, "Thanks, Joe."

CHAPTER THIRTEEN

Debbie has the Yellow Pages on the passenger seat of her car with the book open to stock brokerage firms. She drives by a brokerage office and looks in its window. There is only one man, and he's sitting at a puny desk while he smokes a cigarette and stares out into space.

Debbie continues to drive around the area looking for an office that makes her feel as if it is the right place for her to invest her savings. The Yellow Pages already has five offices crossed out, and she's beginning to feel frustrated.

She eventually drives up to an office in one of the nearby towns. From the outside looking in she sees a lot of activity, and there are both men and women sitting at the broker's desks. All the people who work inside are talking either to customers or on the telephone. Debbie smiles, parks the car, puts on lipstick, and gets out.

An attractive well-dressed woman in her late thirties greets Debbie. "Can I help you?"

"Yes, please. I'm looking for someone to give me money advice."

The woman cordially inquires, "Do you mean an investment adviser?"

Debbie turns red from embarrassment and replies, "Yes."

The broker can see she's feeling uncomfortable and asks her, "What's your name, sweetheart?"

"Debbie."

"Well Debbie, you can call me Marilyn, and I wish

more women were like you. You know, brave enough to manage their own money."

Debbie answers with the sound of pride in her voice, "Well, thank you."

"I'd love to assist you. I'm a broker and licensed financial planner."

Debbie eagerly offers, "You are? Well, my best friend is an aerospace engineer."

"Is your friend also a woman?"

Debbie blushes when she says, "Silly me, I'm sorry, of course she is."

"Now, Debbie would you like to tell me what your financial goals are?"

"I have this nest egg socked away, and I want to invest it wisely."

"Then why don't you have a seat next to me at my desk."

Debbie follows her lead, and they both sit down. Marilyn puts on a pair of cute eyeglasses and turns on a desk lamp.

Debbie whispers, "Marilyn, there's only one catch, I don't want my husband to ever find out about this money."

"That's a good thing for me to know right up front."

Debbie is curious and asks, "Why?"

Marilyn explains, "So that we don't invest your money in something that pays dividends and reports income to the IRS."

"How do we get around my husband finding out about it?"

"Debbie, you're not the first woman to come to me with this same exact problem."

Debbie feels relieved and answers, "Thank goodness I found you, Marilyn. Do you have a husband?"

"No, but I know about these things."

Debbie is exuberant, "I just had this feeling I came to

the right place. Tell me what I need to do."

Marilyn hands Debbie a piece of paper and a pen so she can write down the instructions, "First, I want you to get a post office box, and that's where we'll mail you your statements."

Debbie looks up from writing to ask, "What about income taxes?"

"Debbie, you only pay taxes when you sell your stock for a profit. So, if you hold on to it ..."

Debbie ends Marilyn's sentence, "No taxes?"

"Correct. Would you like something to drink while I get your paperwork ready?"

Debbie's nerves had gotten to her, and she is feeling thirsty. "Yes, please, a Tab if you don't mind."

Marilyn gets up and comes right back with some papers for Debbie to sign, a cold can of Tab, and a straw. Then she asks her, "What kind of businesses would you like to invest in?"

Debbie looks at her can of soda and asks, "Who makes this stuff?"

Marilyn wonders why she asked and replies, "Coca Cola Corporation."

"Great, that's my first choice." And then Debbie gulps down the rest of the can.

"And what would you like for your second choice?"

Debbie wonders why she had to make a second choice as she was perfectly content with her first. She doesn't want to appear stupid in front of Marilyn, but she asks her next question anyway, "When a person returns beer bottles for the deposit money, who takes them away?"

Debbie once again surprises Marilyn with what she perceives as a very intelligent question. "They go back to the bottling plant at the brewery to be washed and refilled. It is an emerging business, and with the recent changes in legislation it has a promising future."

Debbie proudly announces, "Well then, that's my second choice."

"Which brewery would you like?"

"Budweiser!"

Marilyn reaches in the desk drawer for her receipt pad, as she states, "Those are both very interesting choices, I see you like to keep your assets liquid." She chuckles and Debbie doesn't get the joke, so she continues. "How much money will you be investing today?"

Debbie pulls out a large wad of small bills from her pocket. "Here's $1,285.00. I counted it three times, and it's all there."

Marilyn smiles at Debbie, and she doesn't bother to count the money. She writes out the receipt, then hands it to Debbie with a flourish and resists her urge to give Debbie a big congratulatory hug. Debbie's face is beaming with pride when Marilyn respectfully shakes her hand and is thrilled with her client taking the first step toward financial freedom and independence. It was a good day for them both.

CHAPTER FOURTEEN

As Julie pulls up to her driveway in her old station wagon,

Debbie comes out of her house to greet her. Julie gets out

of the car and reaches back inside to collect her heavy

brown leather briefcase and jacket. She is dressed up more

than usual for work, but Debbie doesn't notice the change

in Julie's attire. Just as she also neglects to see the sad

expression on Julie's face.

Debbie announces with the sound of enthusiasm in her voice, "Thank goodness you're home early. I've got to talk to you!"

Julie closes the car door and huffs as she thinks about how all she wanted to do was go inside and kick off her shoes. Dealing tonight with Debbie's ebullient personality after the horrible day she had at work does not appeal to her. As Debbie and Julie walk toward Julie's house, Julie cringes at the sudden noise coming from inside. There's loud rock and roll music blasting from the boy's bedroom. They placed a speaker in the window and have the volume turned up all the way. The song playing is *Purple Sky* and they want to hear it from the roof of the garage.

Debbie grimaces before she suggests, "Can we talk over at my house?"

"Sure, as long as you pour me a stiff drink. I had a long and crummy day."

The minute Julie enters Debbie's house, she kicks off her fancy black patent leather high heels and makes herself comfortable on the couch. Debbie goes into the kitchen and comes back with two tall drinks in sweaty glasses. Debbie places them on coasters and sits down in the easy chair next to the couch. Julie's book, *The Feminine Mystique* is on the coffee table next to the drinks.

Debbie is excited as she points to the glasses and says, "This was the new fancy drink they were serving at the country club."

Julie takes a big gulp and remarks, "It's delicious. What is it?"

"It's called a Harvey Wall Banger."

Julie takes another big swig and asks, "What did you want to talk about?"

"I finished reading the book."

Julie is curious. "What did you think?"

Debbie blushes before she speaks, "I can't believe I'm telling you this." Then she stops talking.

Julie tries to coax it out of her, "You know you can tell me anything."

Debbie puts her face in her hands for a moment and then looks up to speak, "Do you remember when Joe and I went to the big Christmas party at the country club a while back, and we sat with Joe's boss and his wife?"

Julie thinks about it for moment and replies, "Yeah."

Tears formed in Debbie's eyes when she said, "Well, that night people kept asking Joe and me when we're going to start a family."

"So, what did you tell them?"

Debbie reveals, "Nothing. I went in the ladies' room and cried. After that night, I wanted to commit suicide because I felt so worthless." Debbie turns her face away from Julie and can no longer hold back her tears.

Julie doesn't know what to say at first and tries to console her friend, "I'm sorry, Debbie, I had no idea about this. I always thought you and Joe didn't want kids."

Debbie says emphatically, "Want them! I've always wanted a baby and in the worst way. The problem is we can't seem to be able to make one."

Julie inquires softly, "Have you talked to a doctor?"

Debbie answers angrily, "Of course! I've seen three so far, and they all agree there's nothing wrong with me."

Julie concludes, "So, it must be Joe."

Debbie sounds disgusted when she reveals how she truly feels. "The only reason I've ever let that three-hundred-pound gorilla touch me was to get me pregnant."

Julie looks up at the ceiling and asks a rhetorical question, "What are we going to do?" Then she finishes her drink and motions for another. Debbie gets up from her chair and fetches two more tall drinks from the pitcher of Harvey Wall Bangers on the kitchen counter.

While Debbie is in the kitchen preparing the drinks,

Julie has a flashback to the first time she and Stanley had

sex in the back of his mother's 1950 woody station wagon.

Her entire life's destiny was because the moon was full, the

night was hot, and the movie too long; and how all of that

brought her to this exact moment. It happened during the

scene when Moses cast down the Ten Commandments and

God opened the earth, so that all the evil people would fall

into the crevice. That was when Julie succumbed to Stanley

and her own desires and that's when they conceived their

first child.

Debbie returns with two more drinks and raises her

voice when she questions, "What did you mean by we

when you said what are we going to do?"

Julie shrugs her shoulders and replies, "I'm not sure."

Then Julie looks at her drink and huffs.

That's when Debbie realizes that Julie is upset about

something, and she tries to be encouraging, "Your husband

adores you! You have the sweetest children and an exciting career." As she can't imagine what Julie could possibly be thinking because as far as she's concerned, she has it all.

"The only part that's true is the kids." Julie chugs down her second drink before she elaborates. "At work today I did something foolish; I submitted a proposal for the Abort Guidance System. They'll never pick my design." Julie swirls the ice around in her glass feeling sorry for herself. "I could hear them snickering about me when I left the office tonight, and as for Stanley, I'm not in love with him and never was."

This information surprises Debbie. "I thought you two were a perfect match."

"Debbie, Stanley got me pregnant in the back of an old station wagon while we were in college, and that's the only reason why I married him."

Debbie gathers, "That's as good as any other."

Julie moans, "I believe there's got to be more to it, and

practically every time Stanley screws me, he gets me pregnant. What fun is in that?"

Debbie blushes before she replies, "But, Julie, you've still have so much more than me. I've no education, and I feel like I'm worthless."

Julie argues, "Stop talking that way."

"Well, we both know it's the truth. After I finished your book," Debbie taps on it. "I realized my entire life was stolen from me."

Julie agrees, "We both married too young." Then she finishes her drink, and Debbie watches her as she plays with the ice and sulks,

Debbie is also a bit tipsy and confesses, "I've never been with anyone else."

Her comment confuses Julie, and she asks, "Besides Joe, you mean?"

Debbie nods yes and asks, "What about you?"

"Just Stanley."

Debbie complains, "I feel like I'm suffocating. What are you going to do about your marriage?"

Julie looks at the worn thin gold band on her finger and twists it around and around in silence for a moment. Then she looks over at Debbie and admits, "I've been asking myself the same question for a while."

Just then the doorbell rings, and they're both startled. Debbie hollers in a half-drunk stupor, "It's open, come on in."

Stanley enters the living room and finds Debbie and Julie drunk on Harvey Wall Bangers.

Julie sounds obnoxious when she asks, "What do you want, Stanley?"

Stanley is hurt and replies, sounding truly concerned, "I was worried, so I went to find you."

"Debbie invited me in for a drink. I had a rough day, so I accepted her hospitality."

Stanley appears unappreciated when he lists all the chores he completed, "I fed the kids, Matthew and David are practicing their instruments, and Sara's getting ready for bed."

Julie realizes she had hurt his feelings and tries to make amends when she half-heartedly says, "Stanley, you're the best." Then she staggers a little when she gets up to leave Debbie's house.

#

Later that evening, Stanley comes out from their bathroom in his robe and sits on the edge of the bed. Julie walks over to him before she speaks. "Stanley, I can't complain about you. You're an amazing father, friend, and husband."

Stanley didn't anticipate being blindsided and innocently replies, "Thanks, Julie. I feel the same way about you." Then he reaches down to take off his slippers.

Julie continues, "Despite this, I have a problem."

Stanley's puzzled. "I beg your pardon?"

She rubs her chin with her right thumb and paces a bit while she decides what to say next. Then she turns to him and speaks. "Stanley, I'm not happy with our marriage, and I don't know how to say what I want to say."

Stanley stammers, "Are you asking me for a divorce?"

Julie puts both of her hands over her mouth and stands in silence while she determines how far she is willing to go and then she replies, "Yes."

Stanley bursts into tears before he stutters, "Is there someone else?"

The alcohol makes her think fuzzy. She wonders for a moment if this entire conversation is all because of the booze, or if she is speaking her mind about how she really feels. She realizes that Stanley is building up to a rage, so she answers him right away, "No, I swear on our children there isn't someone else. It's just that I believe we'll both be happier apart."

Stanley pleads with her, "You're drunk! I think you'll

feel differently in the morning."

She cuts him off and defends her actions, "That's what gave me the courage to speak my mind tonight."

"We'll talk after you sober up."

Stanley gets into bed hurt and upset. He pulls the covers up to his neck and turns his back to her. Julie picks up her pillow and hugs it while deciding where she should spend the night. Then she pushes the dog off the ratty old throw on the end of bed and grabs it on her way to the living room sofa.

PART TWO

CHAPTER FIFTEEN

Julie had difficulty sleeping on the lumpy living room sofa.

Her bloodshot eyes are glazed over from her Harvey Wall

Banger hangover, and she wonders how she is going to get

through her workday. While she waits for the elevator, she

leans against the cool granite wall hoping for some relief

from the queasiness. She isn't sure if it was from drinking

too much alcohol the night before with Debbie, or if she

has a nervous stomach from telling Stanley she wants a divorce. When the elevator door opens, Julie's eyes subconsciously follow the woman exiting it. This causes the woman to turn around and look back at Julie in response to her uncomfortably long stare. Julie hesitates before going into the elevator. As she watches the door close before she has enough time to enter it, she realizes the woman is waiting for her to say something. There is nowhere for Julie to flee, so after the awkward moment passes, Julie speaks up and asks, "If I'm not mistaken, aren't you Fanny Gold?"

The woman seems stunned when she hears her name. "I haven't heard myself called that in a couple of years." After a short pause to collect her thoughts she offers her married name, "It's Fanny Stone now, and who are you?"

"Fanny, it's me, Julie Levine, from Brooklyn."

"Shut up! You can't be! I never imagined running into someone from Brooklyn way out here in California."

Julie feigns ignorance, "So, do you work here?"

Fanny confirms what Julie already knows, "I'm in the typing pool for now. What about you?"

Julie boasts, "I'm an aerospace engineer."

Fanny's face looks genuinely stunned, and for a second Julie could swear she saw a flash of seething jealousy. Fanny quickly looks down at Julie's hand before she states in a mean tone, "And you've time for a husband as well. Good lord, I never thought you'd get married."

Julie never liked Fanny Gold or her best friend Betty Ann Abramowitz; she remembered them as being cruel and shallow girls. They were such phonies back then, and she wondered if anything had changed. Julie looks at her, and guesses she had nothing more than a charm school degree, and wonders if she ever regretted not taking her education more seriously. Those girls had taunted her for being motivated, but it was Julie's turn to shine, so she remarks, "I have three wonderful children. What about you?"

At this point Fanny turns green with envy, and she angrily retorts, "We're still waiting for the stork."

Julie glances at Fanny's ID badge and thinks about the last name. Then she makes a comment based on her earlier observation. "What was the name Stone before it was changed? Was it Stein perhaps?"

Fanny is forthcoming with her personal information. "Oh, that. We're both Christians, I converted, and my husband's last name was always just plain old Stone." Fanny looks Julie up and down before she forces her next words out of her mouth through clenched teeth. "We should get together for dinner sometime soon and bring our husbands."

Julie feels a bit embarrassed by this innocuous request because the last thing in the world she would be able to make was a date for dinner that included Stanley, and soon enough everyone around the office would know that she was about to become a "divorced woman". Julie answers with a simple reply, "We should." Then she repeatedly

presses the elevator button and escapes from that awful

conversation to the sanctuary of the empty elevator.

Julie walks quickly to her tiny windowless office and

closes the door behind her. A couple of minutes pass and

there is a knock at the door. Julie grabs a stack of papers

and pretends to be at work when she responds, "Come in."

Penny enters and sits down across from Julie. "What's

up, boss? You're not yourself today."

Julie's face flushes before she makes her request in

earnest, "Can you keep this between us?"

Penny answers, "I've never repeated anything you've

ever told me."

Julie blurts, "Stanley's moving out!"

Penny is in shock when she says, "Holy cow!" Then

Penny stands up from her chair and walks over to Julie. She

places her hands on Julie's shoulders because Julie has

begun to cry, and she tries to comfort her. Then she asks a very personal question, "Is it another woman?"

Julie wipes the tears from her eyes and explains, "No, I told him that I don't love him, so he packed his stuff this morning and went out to look for an apartment nearby."

Penny remarks, "That sounds painful."

Julie continues, "The last thing I want to do is hurt him."

Penny says with a quiver in her voice, "I think you may have crushed him."

Julie places her head on her desk and continues to cry. That's when Penny pats her on the back and hands her a tissue. "Here, take this and clean yourself up."

When Julie looks up, her mascara is smudged, and it is running down her face. At that moment it occurs to her that Penny had knocked on her door for a reason, so she inquires, "You came in to see me. What did you want?" Then she places her heavy head back on her desk while she listens to Penny's reply.

"Remember Susie who was having an affair with Fred?"

Julie uncaringly responds, "Yeah."

Penny continues to share the office gossip, "Well, can you believe he left his wife and kids for her?"

"No way, I never would have believed it in a million years!" This news truly stuns Julie, and she raises her weary head to listen eagerly to the details of the gossip.

Penny could see this was distracting Julie from her own troubles and cheered her up a bit, "They're getting married soon; word is Susie's pregnant, so tonight at The Tiki Hut is her bridal/baby shower. You know that place off the highway with the huge umbrella drinks."

Julie confesses, "I love that place."

"Do you want to come along? It's just us girls from the office."

Julie cringes at the thought of being around them while going through a divorce. "No, I don't think so. I'm too depressed, but thanks for asking me."

#

At the Tiki Hut later that same day the girls are seated at a very long, ridiculously decorated table, and while waiting for the Pu Pu platters to arrive, they're sipping their enormous Polynesian drinks and smoking cigarettes. Penny is directly across from Fanny and next to nosy Linda, Joshua's secretary. There are about 15 women, and at that point in the evening almost everyone is tipsy. Penny is an exception because she arrived late and has not ordered her drink yet.

Fanny mutters, in a matter-of-fact way while sipping from her Scorpion Bowl, "I can't get believe that Julie Levine works here."

Her comment perks Linda's interest, and she inquires, "How do you know her?"

Fanny brags to the group like she's friends with a celebrity, "We went to high school together."

Just then Penny's Mai Tai arrives. It was at that instant

she realizes who sat down next to her, and she straightens up in her chair so she can pay closer attention to what Fanny has to say about Julie.

Fanny asks the group, "Does Julie still hang all over the boys?"

Linda is quick to remark, "Well, I've noticed she can get a little too close to Joshua."

Fanny embellishes, "Oh my goodness, some things never change. She hung out with three boys at a time back in high school."

Linda jumps right in with zest, "I've seen Julie in Joshua's office with the door closed for hours on end. God knows what they're doing in there?"

Fanny contributes, "You know what that means." Then she takes a big swig of her drink and rolls her eyes.

Linda taps her drink against Fanny's; it was as if she were making a toast. "I've had my suspicions." She elaborates.

Fanny's voice grows louder as she becomes more inebriated, "I wouldn't put it past her to have an affair with a guy from the office."

Susie lifts her silly-looking, make-believe wedding veil and glares at Fanny. Then Susie sneers at her for making a comment like that at her shower, which only reminds everyone about her interoffice affair with Fred. The rest of the women at the table have overheard Fanny's accusation, and they begin to whisper to one another. Fanny has infuriated Penny so much that she stands up, grabbing her handbag at the same time and without uttering a word, she tosses down a ten-dollar bill and walks out the door.

Fanny asks with slurred speech as she shouts across the restaurant to Penny, "Hey you, what's your problem?"

Penny doesn't turn around or bother to reply to her.

Everyone else at the table remains quiet until she's gone.

Florence turns to Fanny and raises her voice, "Her problem is simply this; she's Julie's secretary and also her closest friend at work." Then Florence collects her purse, hat, gloves and follows Penny out the door.

CHAPTER SIXTEEN

Julie burst into Joshua's office without knocking on the half-open door and closes it behind her. Joshua looks up at her as she announces, "Pack your bags, we're flying to Houston."

Joshua's first thought is she's kidding but goes along with what he thinks is a charade. So, he asks her, "When?"

She offers more details. "This Sunday afternoon, if that's all right."

Joshua says in jest, "Sounds great. What's our mission?"

Julie boasts with a beaming smile, "The engineers at NASA want to go over my design for the Abort Guidance System."

Joshua is genuinely shocked. "No way! They picked yours over everyone else's. That will make you the Project Manager."

"Yes and no. Yes, they picked my proposal, and no, they won't promote me to project manager, but they're willing to go ahead with my design if you're my co-manager and will deal with all the red tape."

Joshua wants to know, "What kind of red tape?"

"They want you to sign off on expenses, payroll, and the internal technical stuff that they don't trust a woman with." She smirks.

He huffs, "What a bunch of morons! You were the only one who could figure how to make the AGS run on a digital computer, and they don't think you're capable of adding up overtime hours."

Julie concurs with him, "Exactly."

He sneers before he displays a wolfish grin, "Wow, the timing couldn't be any stranger for us."

She asks, "What do you mean?

"I guess you haven't heard?" He stands from his chair and walks over to her. She can feel the hairs on the back of her neck rise as he walks around her.

"Nope, I haven't, but I hope it's hot and steamy." He is face to face with her and she can smell the scent of his intoxicatingly spicy cologne. Her body trembles with excitement.

He reveals, "Oh, it's very hot, and it's steamy all right. Except, this time it's about us."

Julie is titillated when she cries out, "No way!"

He lowers his voice when he says, "The talk around the office is you left Stanley for me."

They're eye to eye when she reacts to his comment and blurts, "You've got to be kidding me."

Joshua backs off when he repeats, "That's the word around here."

Julie asks jokingly, "So, is there any truth to it?"

Joshua leans in and is almost close enough to kiss her, but instead he slowly moves his lips to her ear, and his hot breath gives her goose bumps. Then he whispers, "If you don't mind, I'd prefer if you wouldn't deny it."

This information confuses her, but she says, "Okay," and intentionally leaves her ear near his lips.

Cautiously he begins to explain. "People are suspicious about why I've never married."

The sudden change in his tone breaks the spell he had over her, and Julie backs away from him. "Joshua, I've never seen you with anyone less than the most beautiful girl in the room."

"I know, but I'm a little too old to be a bachelor, and

that makes some people a bit uncomfortable around me at work."

Julie smiles when she reiterates, "Well, you just haven't met the right girl yet, that's all."

Joshua hoped Julie would be more receptive to what he is trying to explain to her, but she simply replies, "If you say so."

She adds, "You're such a ladies' man, and I don't know anyone who can dance better than you can." and this makes him feel defeated in his quest.

He sounds disappointed when he answers, "Thanks for the compliment. You do understand this trip will be as good as a confession from us."

Julie perks up, "I really don't give a crap what the hens are clucking about in the typing pool."

#

Julie is so excited about going away with Joshua on a business trip that she can't contain herself. It's the night before they're to leave for Houston, she finds herself pacing up and down the aisles of a busy drugstore. She is startled when she hears the pharmacist announce her name over the loudspeaker followed by, "Your birth control pills are ready for pick up." Julie is mortified by the embarrassment of everyone in the drugstore knowing what she is there to buy. She looks at the back door and thinks about leaving immediately without the pills but decides to collect them first, because she thinks she's really going to need them. She waits in the shadows until there are no more people left. As the pharmacist hands her the birth control pills, she looks left and right to make sure no one recognizes her.

The pharmacist asks, "Do you have any questions about your new prescription?"

She quickly shakes her head no, grabs the pills, and tosses a twenty-dollar bill on the counter. Then she dashes out the back door of the drugstore without bothering to

collect her change.

CHAPTER SEVENTEEN

Their flight to Houston is on a medium-sized prop plane
with the seats configured in rows of two on both sides of
the aisle. Julie sits by the window with Joshua next to her.
When the plane levels off, she immediately reclines her
seat and reaches for her TWA flight bag in search of
something to read. That's when she notices that her TWA
flight bag that came with their tickets is identical to

Joshua's, and they're placed side by side on the floor in front of them.

Her ears are plugged from the change in cabin pressure, so she finds it difficult to hear the handsome steward speak to them. He is standing in front of the cart for drinks, food, and cigarettes, and since they're free, they're especially difficult for Joshua to resist. Julie watches the steward, as he prepares the drinks for the people across the aisle from them. She takes a second look at him because she finds him to be an exceptionally handsome man in a stylish sort of way; nice haircut, clean nails, spicy aftershave. He glances over at Julie and Joshua and smiles at them. The flash of his remarkable white teeth is penetrating, and his good looks make her feel a bit flushed.

He politely asks Joshua, "Would your wife like a drink?"

Joshua responds in a flirtatious manner, "She's not my wife, she's, my boss."

Julie is intrigued by Joshua's quick response and believes his explanation is for her benefit to make her appear more interesting to the steward. What a sweet gesture she considers, as she twists her wedding ring around her finger and makes eye contact with the handsome man.

He repeats the question, "And what would you like to drink, mam?"

Julie just doesn't want a drink; she feels as if she needs one and she can sense her heart racing as if she's having a panic attack. She's "flying solo" for the very first time in her life, and she hopes the liquor will help steady her jitters. She is just beginning to realize what solo is and is concerned over the silliest of things, as she batts her long brown eyelashes at the steward and thinks about the never used before birth control pills in her purse. Then she raises her voice and requests. "A screwdriver, please."

The steward shows her a small Smirnoff and she nods

yes, and he behaves as if he doesn't notice her flirtations at all. He hands her the drink without pause, but when he turns to Joshua, his face turns to a soft pink glow right before he inquires, "And for you, sir?"

Joshua tucks his right hand into the waist of his pants while considering his choices. "Mmmm, a screwdriver sounds like a great idea. I just happen to like a good screwdriver every so often, and by the way, I'm not married, how about you?"

Julie is feeling self-conscious and can't get over Joshua's intrusive inquiry about this guy's personal life. She can't imagine any other reason than Joshua's trying to hook her up with the steward after they land in Huston, but she's not feeling she's ready yet. She worries about what she might say and she's afraid telling a new guy she has three kids will turn him off. Overwhelmed with insecurity she doesn't bother to listen any further and reaches for the warmed mixed nuts and devours them. Then she pulls out an issue of *Popular Mechanics* from her TWA flight bag and begins to read it and doesn't bother to listen to the conversation going on between the two men. In addition, her hearing has not yet returned from the drop in cabin pressure, so she misses the comment to Joshua when the steward whispers to him, "You're a lot of fun, aren't you?" and doesn't notice right after that he reaches in his cart and grabs a handful of vodka and scotch nips before he quietly adds, "Here take these along with you."

"Refills anyone?" the steward inquires.

Joshua replies, "Why not," but Julie ignores the question entirely and continues to read.

The steward returns to refill Joshua's drink and hangs around to chat with him. Nothing about it strikes Julie as unusual, and she continues to ignore them.

Joshua asks him, "Where are you based?"

"Dallas, but tonight we're doing our layover in Houston.

I had to cover for someone at the last minute, so this isn't my regular route."

Joshua smiles when he says, "Lucky me."

Just then the seat belt sign illuminates, and the captain announces their descent into Houston.

The steward is grinning while he checks the passengers' seat belts on his return to his jump seat.

#

The hotel is so close to the airport that it takes less than two minutes to get to the Sheraton after picking up the rental car from Avis. The valet whisks the car away, and Julie barely has enough time to recall if the boxy Chrysler was gray or blue. The bellhop collects their suitcases, briefcases, and identical flight bags and off he goes.

Julie feels the need to take charge of matters because she's trying to ease into her new role as project manager, so she offers to check them into their rooms. Joshua doesn't care one way or the other and heads straight to the bar where he orders them another round of drinks.

The bar was bustling with businessmen. When Julie enters, all eyes, including the bartender's, are on her. She is the only female in the place except for the bleach-blond, middle-aged cocktail waitress whose clothing is so provocative it's almost too obvious that she is wearing it to help her hustle for bigger tips, but no one is complaining. When Julie sits next to Joshua, she doesn't notice the disappointed looks on the other men's faces on either side of them, but he does because he's much more situationally aware than she is.

Julie looks around the bar as if she were inspecting the merchandise. That's when Joshua motions to get the bartender's attention, and then turns to Julie and chastises her, "Take off the damn thing!"

"What are you referring to, Joshua?" she innocently replies.

He says from out of the side of his mouth, "Your

wedding ring. Your divorce is almost final, and it's time for you to jump back in the pool."

Julie takes a big gulp of her drink before she responds, "Well, for your information, I've never been in the pool before and I'm not sure if I know how to swim anymore."

Joshua apologizes to her, "Sorry to hear that."

Julie nervously inquires, "So, are you going to teach me?"

Joshua looks at her up and down, as if he were seeing her for the first time in his life. Then he gives a lot of thought to his advice before he offers it to her, "Well, for starters, take off the wedding ring! It's a real turnoff for most guys."

Julie follows his directions and tosses her wedding ring in her purse and snaps it shut. She squirms on the bar stool while she waits for his next bit of advice. He sits there with his drink in his hand while thinking, so she urges him to continue, "Then what?"

Joshua breaks his silence with more words of wisdom. "Find out if there's a hair salon nearby and make an appointment for first thing tomorrow morning."

Julie touches her hand to her hair when she asks, "Is it that bad?"

Joshua frowns, "It looks as if you've been cutting it yourself."

Julie takes his criticism of her on the chin and pulls out a tube of pink lipstick from her purse. While applying it, she notices in the reflection of the tiny cosmetic mirror the handsome steward from their flight walking into the bar. She's excited when she points him out to Joshua and says, "Isn't that …?"

Joshua cuts her off, "By golly, it is!" He waves to get his attention. Julie moves over to the next stool to make room for him and is feeling elated. The steward stands behind the empty barstool and waits for an invitation to take a seat.

Joshua sounds thrilled when he says, "Hey, buddy, what are you doing here?" Then winks at him.

The dashing young man simply replies with an elated smile, "Looking for you."

Joshua grins when he offers him a drink while motioning for the bartender's attention once again and then he proclaims, "Our tab is courtesy of the United States of America." Then he smirks.

Joshua's handsome friend orders champagne and confesses, "I feel like celebrating tonight." He picks up his glass, stares into Joshua's eyes, and says, "Cheers!"

Meanwhile, Julie is carrying on a conversation with a well-dressed businessman who is sitting to her immediate right. She's just finished explaining to him that she is not married to Joshua, and that they work together. That's when she turns to her left to introduce her acquaintance, only to discover both Joshua and the handsome steward from their flight have vanished, but there is a wad of cash left on the bar right in front of where Joshua had been sitting.

Her new friend notices they took off on her and announces, "I'm so glad I happened to run into a pretty lady the likes of you, Julie."

His comment is exactly the kind of thing she was in the mood to hear, and she finds his South-West accent cute. Julie is flattered, and Joshua's disappearance doesn't bother her at all. She is actually somewhat relieved he's gone. The thought of life throwing them together like this has frightened her, and the last thing she ever wants to do is jeopardize their wonderful relationship over something as meaningless as a fling, even though she had seriously entertained the idea on several occasions. She turns to the man sitting next to her and replies, "Well, thank you."

She calls over to the bartender and requests the check and insists that her new friend's bar tab is on her.

The bartender turns around from counting the pile of money left behind by Joshua and exclaims, "You're all set and thank you so much!"

Her acquaintance turns to face her and inquires, "How about joining me for a big, thick, juicy steak?"

Julie is fairly inebriated at this point, and except for the garnish in her drinks and some warm nuts on the airplane, she hadn't eaten anything all day. She thinks about her choices of eating a sandwich alone in the room or having a night out on the town and answers, "Why the hell not?"

He gentlemanly holds out his arm for her and escorts her to the door. It isn't her dream date but it's the perfect place for her to break the ice and she's having a nice time.

Later that same evening after a wonderful steak dinner with Charlie from Oklahoma, Julie is back in her room and restless. It's probably the two cups of coffee and chocolate cake for dessert, but before their appetizers arrived, she already knew there was no chemistry between them. Being so far away from home, they were both grateful to have company for dinner. He was also newly divorced and missed his kids. He explained how the time he spent working on the road probably cost him his marriage. By the main course, they were sharing photos of their children. She made a note to herself that not only is wearing one's wedding ring a turnoff to men, so is talking all night about the kids and ex-spouse.

The noise from the next room of people having loud sex is annoying her. She walks over to the adjoining room door and is about to bang on it, but she hesitates and decides to turn on the TV to mask it. She watches *Star Trek* for a few seconds, and instantly realizes it's a rerun. She's anxious over her upcoming meeting in the morning at NASA. She stands up again and rummages through her TWA flight bag. She hopes that finishing the article she started earlier in the day will help her relax. She's surprised when she reaches down and feels a couple of tiny bottles. They're the nips of vodka and scotch from the flight in. She reaches

down a second time and feels some magazines buried at the

bottom of the flight bag and underneath them is a cassette

recorder that doesn't belong to her. Realizing this is not her

bag she guiltily pulls out all the magazines in search of

anything decent to read and throws them on the bed. Her

eyes open wide as pies as she spies a pile of male porn

magazines with explicit photos of handsome naked men in

provocative poses. She immediately finds them interesting

and sits on her bed with a vodka straight up, poured into the

bathroom's water glass while she closely examines each

page. The TV continues to play *Star Trek* in the

background, but she doesn't notice it any longer, as the

noise from people having sex in the adjoining room

rockets.

CHAPTER EIGHTEEN

The next morning, Julie follows Joshua's instructions to the

letter. She gets up early to have her hair done and spends

time on her wardrobe choices. She returns to the hotel with

a chic new hairstyle. Her hair color is brighter, and her

already pretty face looks exceptionally beautiful. Julie is

finally transformed into the attractive, self-confident

woman she was destined to become. As she gets off the

elevator on her floor, she sees Joshua and the steward from their flight coming out of the room next to hers. The elevator door is already closed behind her, so she ducks into the shadow of a nearby doorway down the hall. As the steward passes her, she turns away and pretends to open the door.

She waits for Joshua to close the door to his room, and then she goes into her room to change before leaving for their 10:45 meeting with the people from NASA. She glances at her watch and notes they have plenty of time. She's nervous about meeting Andy Kennedy, the head of operations, and wonders about what she should wear. Just thinking about the meeting gives her tingles. A part of her still can't believe that out of all the designs at her company they picked hers to go to the moon. Just at that exact moment, the thought of Mrs. Temple handing her that college prep math book pops into her head, and she can't help feeling that if it weren't for her former teacher's encouragement none of this ever would have happened.

Julie looks at herself in the mirror and likes what she sees. She puts on a crisp white shirt and a beautiful full wool skirt that makes her waist look extra trim. She appears more like the girl showing off the car of the future at the auto show than an aerospace engineer about to embark on one of the most sophisticated projects in the history of humankind. She giggles and wonders if her father was still feeling a little bit ripped off for not having any sons. Then she thinks about calling her sister in New York and decides that it would sound like bragging, so she doesn't.

She repacks everything she took out of the flight bag the night before and places it next to her briefcase. She applies another coat of lipstick, blots it with a tissue just like Penny taught her and makes her way to Joshua's hotel room door. When she knocks on it, there is no answer.

#

Julie goes down to the lobby to find Joshua and notices him through the window standing out front next to the rental car waiting for her. As she steps outside, he pleads, "Julie darling, would you mind driving this morning? I didn't sleep a wink last night."

Julie smiles at him before she announces, "First things first. I need to give you back your flight bag." She hands it to him and watches his facial expression change quickly as he begins to blush. Then she asks, "Did you realize that we have adjoining rooms?"

Joshua pretends to be aloof, "No I did not." Then the tone in his voice changes; it sounds panicked when he asks, "Are you going to drive us or what?"

Julie acquiesces, "Okay, get in."

When they are both in the car, it is obvious that Joshua is going to be of no help with navigating. She glances at her handwritten directions while driving and adjusting the rear-view mirror at the same time. Eventually, she pulls out onto the highway and heads in the right direction.

They come to the first sign directing them to the Manned Space Center. That's when Joshua finally breaks the silence. "By the way, your hair came out amazing, and I see you put your wedding ring back on."

Julie defends her actions. "I think the ring makes me look more like a serious professional." She nervously touches her hair as she looks in the review mirror. Julie then changes the subject so she can deal with the uncomfortable moment caused by her recent discovery in the TWA travel bag. She states, "I must apologize to you, Joshua."

"For what?" he asks.

"I've been as shallow as a puddle. I consider you one of my closest friends, and I don't know the first thing about you."

He grins before he says, "I don't have a problem with that."

Julie continues, "How about that it never occurred to me that you're a homosexual?"

"Well, you've been a busy little beaver, and I haven't exactly shared that part of my life with you."

Julie continues, "That's no excuse."

Joshua smirks, "Julie, it's not your fault. Let me demonstrate to you how it happened."

"How are you going to do that?"

Joshua runs his fingers through his thick head of black hair and looks out the window for a moment. Then he turns to her to explain, "You're walking through life with your eyes closed, seeing what other people want you to see."

She snaps back with, "It's hard for me to agree with you, but go ahead."

Joshua reaches into his TWA flight bag and pulls out a cassette recorder. "I brought this in case there weren't any decent radio stations down here." Joshua turns on the car radio and twists the dial. All the stations are classic-country music, so he turns the radio off.

She exclaims, "My hero! What did you bring for us to listen to in the car?"

Joshua turns the cassette recorder on. It's music from *My Fair Lady* and the song playing is, *I Could Have Danced All Night*.

Julie chuckles, "Nice choice, and I think you did dance all night."

"Not quite. I got about an hour of sleep, but it was worth it."

Julie asks, "What else is on the tape?"

"There's music from *West Side Story* and *The King and I*. He fast-forwards to the song, *Somewhere* from *West Side Story*. Then he asks her, "Julie, my love, who is singing this song?"

Julie thinks this is a truly stupid question and answers, "Natalie Wood, of course!"

Then he inquires, "And who sang the last song I

played?"

Julie loves to play trivia games and wants to know some details before she responds to the question, "Was that the Broadway show with Julie Andrews or the film with Audrey Hepburn?"

"It is the film version."

"Then it must have been Audrey's voice."

Joshua taps on the cassette recorder when he says, "What if I told you that you were wrong twice?"

Julie becomes upset and asserts, "I own these records, and I've read the credits on the cover carefully. I'm right."

Joshua pulls out the cassette tape and shows it to her. "My ex-boyfriend was the sound engineer on those albums, and I was let in on one of the biggest secrets in Hollywood."

Julie giggles and asks sarcastically, "So, are you going to share this gigantic secret with me?"

Joshua spells it out for her. "Marni Nixon sang every song on this cassette."

She asks, "Who is Marni Nixon?"

He boasts, "Marni Nixon is one of the best singers to ever live."

"Oh, please. Now I know you're full of it. How did you hear this bull crap?"

"From my friends. Did you know there's an entire underground network of us?"

She's confused. "What do you mean by us?"

He replies, "I'm talking about men like me. Did you know that there are homosexuals everywhere?"

"There are? I never gave it much thought."

"For example, Leonard Bernstein and his choreographer are a homosexual couple, and so is the set designer of My Fair Lady."

Julie argues, "Now I know you're nuts. Leonard Bernstein is married with kids. I saw photos of his family in

Life magazine."

Joshua responds, "Do you know where I've been vacationing?"

She feels embarrassed again by his question. "I can't believe it, but I don't."

"Fire Island and Leonard's there every Memorial Day with his lover. That's where guys like us go in the summer."

As they approach the Manned Space Center in Houston, Joshua's mood turns somber. He looks away from Julie and confesses. "You've no idea how much weight has lifted off me. I've wanted to share this part of my life with you for so many years, but I was too afraid to tell you." Joshua starts to cry tears of relief.

Julie places her hand over his and squeezes it. Then she acknowledges her feelings for him when she says, "I love you, Joshua, and I will always love you."

CHAPTER NINETEEN

At NASA's Manned Space Center in Houston, a young

male intern greets Julie and Joshua in the lobby. He easily

identifies them from their photo ID badges, plus Julie is

one of the only woman in the lobby, and as he welcomes

them, he hands over their badges to them. Then he requests

they follow him. They pass by a portrait of President

Johnson hung in the middle of a shiny, gray, granite wall with a large American flag next to it.

Joshua keeps his Ray Bans on to disguise his fatigue as he struggles with the fast pace. After an arduously long walk, they reach a doorway where the nameplate reads "Andy Kennedy, Director of Operations." The intern knocks and steps back. A tall, older woman with short blond hair emerges from the office; she stops at the threshold and places her hands on her hips. She takes a second to look over Joshua and Julie. Then she says ceremoniously, "Welcome to the Manned Space Center - Follow me."

Julie appears disappointed and confused, so Joshua nudges to ask her why. Julie does not have enough time to respond before the woman motions for them to speed up the pace. When she is a few steps ahead of them, Julie can whisper to Joshua, "What happened to Kennedy?"

Just then another man in uniform catches up with them

from behind. All three stop, so the woman guiding the tour can turn around to talk to him. He has a clipboard that he hands over to her. He's still out of breath when he offers her a pen and breathlessly states, "Mrs. Kennedy, I'm so glad I caught up with you. I forgot to have you sign this urgent document before you left for your next meeting." Joshua jabs Julie in the arm and smiles at her for making her earlier assumption regarding Andy Kennedy's gender.

Andy Kennedy makes an announcement that sounds more like a proclamation than an apology to Julie and Joshua. "I'm so sorry about the interruption. I know you must be eager to get started with your project." Joshua is grateful for the respite, so he can catch his breath.

Julie and Joshua follow her, and Joshua smirks at Julie as they make their way toward their destination. Astronauts are in training, wearing-state-of-the-art space suits, pass them as they walk down the bustling and extremely long hallways. The first set of doors is to an ultramodern cafeteria. Julie strains to look inside the enormous room that is overflowing with clean-cut, handsome young men, but they are walking too quickly for her to see much of anything. Then they go by the Neutral Buoyancy Laboratory. Joshua realizes the man coming out from the lab is Buzz Aldrin, and Julie gasps when the famous astronaut brushes by her. Farther down the hallway, they pass by the centrifuge laboratory, but they are disappointed because it is not in operation. Afterwards they pass an Apollo Command Service Module with astronauts training for their upcoming mission. The astronauts are strapped inside the CSM, and in the middle of a mock countdown.

Finally, they reach an oversized set of doors, and the sign reads in large capital letters, LUNAR EXCURSION MODULE LABORATORY. Julie, Joshua, and Andy enter. They pause for a moment while Andy gets everyone's attention. The young engineers are busy at work. They are mostly dressed alike in short-sleeved, white shirts with pocket protectors that hold pens, pencils, and slide rules. They all have thin ties and wear their hair short, and every single one of them is clean-shaven. One man stands out from the rest because his hair is slightly longer and instead of shoes, he's wearing cowboy boots. He's very tall. Julie estimates at least 6' 4", and he is probably close to her age, but she thinks she might be older than him. But what caught her attention more than anything wasn't his height or his great build. It's the sweet sadness emanating from his piercing blue eyes. She focuses a moment longer than she should of on his nametag which reads Sam Brown. And Sam notices it, as he involuntarily makes eye contact with her. After he stares back at her, she realizes what she's done, and she feels self-conscious. With no ability to stop her body's natural reaction, she feels a flash of heat, followed by a rush of embarrassment, and she realizes this is not a great way to start a new project. Andy appears unaware and continues to show them around the laboratory, as if nothing had transpired. Joshua is in such awe of their new workspace that he doesn't pay any attention to Julie at all and only wants to continue the tour. Eventually it ends, and Andy instructs them to plop their belongings down at their assigned workspaces. Then she begins to introduce them to everyone.

The men gather as Andy announces, "Hey all, come 'round so you can meet Julie, your new PM from CA, and her associate engineer, Joshua."

A couple of the aerospace engineers come forward to shake hands and introduce themselves. Apprehensively, Sam Brown remains in the background and watches.

#

Joshua, Julie, and Andy go off to have lunch in the cafeteria and get to know one another. It is so crowded; it takes them a couple of minutes to find three chairs together in the large room. Julie notes that the men in the middle of eating their lunch move aside for them when they reached the table. She concludes it was out of respect for their boss,

Andy Kennedy. After they sit down, Joshua gets up to fill

his coffee cup again. Julie and Andy have a simple lunch of

turkey sandwiches with small cartons of milk on their trays.

Andy confesses in a soft voice, "You caught me off

guard this morning."

Julie inquires, "How's that exactly?"

"Well, I wasn't expecting a woman."

Julie replies sarcastically, "With a name like Julie?"

Andy seems flustered, "Well, I thought it was a Jewish

boy's name, like Jule Styne."

Andy's response confuses Julie, and she asks, "Who?"

"Styne. He's the Jewish fellow who wrote *People*. I'm a

big fan of Barbra's."

Julie finally understands what she meant and realizes

that Andy knows she is Jewish too. Trying to smooth things

over, she says, "Oh, him. His name is short for Julius."

Then she changes the subject. "So how did you end up

running this place?"

Andy is thrilled to share her history with Julie. "I suppose I have Rosie the Riveter to thank."

Julie mumbles while chewing on her sandwich, "Why her?"

"She broke the ice for all of us gals during the big war, and that made it a lot easier for me. There were lots of women back then working in the aerospace industry." Then Andy devours half her sandwich in three big bites.

Julie finds what she said almost impossible to believe and asks sarcastically, "So, where are they now?"

Andy has a scowl on her face when she looks at Julie and angrily states, "Who do you think you are, Enrico Fermi?" Then she angrily bites into the second half of her sandwich, as she tries to calm down. While she chews, she collects herself and begins to explain what happened, "When the men returned from the war, most of the women ran off and got married."

"What happened to you?" Julie instantaneously wishes she could have sucked her question back into her mouth as the words escape her lips.

Andy replies without a pause as she shrugs her broad shoulders, "I was already married, and I loved my work way too much to give it up. What about you?"

Julie is so relieved that her last question didn't insult her. "I'm considered a good problem solver and things like puzzles are easy for me. I won my high school's college scholarship, and afterward a terrific company on the West Coast hired me. They even paid for my graduate school."

Andy smiles when she remarks, "You must be a smarty. You can count all the woman project managers working here on one hand."

Julie makes a self-effacing comment about her intellect, "Thanks, but I think I'm just tenacious."

Andy picks up her small carton of milk and toasts Julie with it.

After Julie puts down her carton of milk, she frowns as she confesses to Andy, "The moon mission has been hardest on my kids."

Andy reminisces about her child-rearing experiences, "I took a couple of years off to raise mine and came back when they started school. Now they're grown and with kids of their own."

"You were lucky to have them when you did. It was much harder for me, she confesses. Each time the Russians moved ahead of us in the space race, my maternity leave was shortened."

Andy nods in agreement with Julie's observation. "I know exactly what you mean, and the pressure has been unbelievable down here also."

Julie complains, "Before Sputnik, it was six weeks paid leave, but after Yuri Gagarin went into space, they cut me down to 10 days for Sara, my youngest." Julie takes her last sip of milk and places the empty carton on the tray. She looks Andy straight in the eye and comments with serious indignation in her voice, "I hate the Russians."

Just then Joshua returns with another cup of coffee and a half-eaten fruit Danish between his teeth. He places his tray on the table next to Julie, sits down to joins the gals. She wonders if he left her alone with Andy to give them some space and appreciates his sensitivity to her needs. He seems hesitant, as if he thought he might be interrupting their ongoing conversation. He attempts to lighten the mood and mutters while still chewing, "The food here is simply scrumptious."

#

That night, Joshua decides to give Julie a break and drive them back to the hotel. It was the end of their first day at NASA, they're haggard and can't believe how far they had to walk to get to everything, but he felt it was unfair of him to ask her to drive the long drive both ways, especially after the grueling mental workout the engineers put her through all afternoon. They tore apart her design and were unmerciful. He estimates they asked her at least a hundred different highly complicated questions about her design. He glances over at her and she's sound asleep with her head bobbing. They questioned the basis of her math model for the Lunar Excursion Module's descent on the moon, and what would happen if the original guidance system failed. They wouldn't let up, and they wanted to know how the backup system would salvage the mission in case of an emergency. If the Guidance System they already had in place failed, they wanted proof this would work in enough time to save the lives of the astronauts onboard, but she shined like a bright star when she demonstrated how the new system would kick in. By the end of the meeting, she had converted them into devoted followers of her plan for the landing mission.

Julie lifts her head from where it's resting against the car's window frame, and she inquisitively taps Joshua on the arm. "I need to ask you something about what you said this morning."

Joshua smiles when he replies, "Sure, what is it?"

"You weren't teasing me, were you?"

"Don't be ridiculous," he criticizes.

Julie confesses, "I'm so gullible. Were you laughing behind my back all day?"

He's feeling disappointed, hurt, and confused and can't understand why she's toying with his feelings, but Julie doesn't understand how fragile he is regarding this matter. She can't know how he is holding back his tears. He raises the pitch in his voice to mask how he feels when he asks her, "About my being a homosexual or Marni Nixon?"

Julie states, "Both."

"True and true."

Julie takes a deep breath and looks out the window at the arid landscape, then turns to him and questions, "What about Barbra?"

He raises his voice another octave when he curiously inquires while choking back his tears, "Streisand?"

"Yes, I meant her. Is she also a fake?"

Joshua laughs with relief at the innocence of Julie's concern, "Nope, she's for real."

"Thank goodness something's are still sacred." She finally relaxes in her seat and closes her tired eyes.

CHAPTER TWENTY

Julie and Joshua are outside the luggage carousel at LAX.
Julie spies Debbie driving up in her white Valiant station
wagon. She waves to her from the crowded curb to get her
attention. Julie's children are jumping with joy on the
backseat when the car comes to a stop in front of her. Julie
leans her head into the back window and kisses her
children. Her oldest son, David, turns his face away when

she stretches toward him, and only allows her to kiss him on the cheek. She immediately notices his facial hair has started to grow in and that he has body odor. Sara is dressed as a pirate with an eye patch, but Matthew is too angry about her being gone so long he doesn't hug her back. He locks his arms across his chest making himself inaccessible.

Julie turns to Joshua and insists, "Come back with us. I'll drive you from my house."

Joshua glances at his watch and replies, "I'm going to grab a cab. There's still enough time left in the day for me to go to the driving range."

Julie kisses him goodbye on the cheek. He catches a passing taxi; tosses his TWA flight bag and suitcase on the seat, jumps in, and waves to her through the open window as the cab drives away.

#

Less than an hour later, Joshua is practicing his swing at the driving range. He is an excellent golfer, and reliably hits his balls farther and farther out. A handsome well-built man in his mid-30s notices the impressive display of Joshua's skill and comments, "Wow, who'd you take lessons from, Arnold Palmer?"

Joshua loves to put on a show, and he hits his next ball even farther. Then he turns to ask, "How about that one?" While he smiles at his audience of one.

The man is genuinely excited when he inquires, "What are you doing this Saturday morning?"

Joshua takes another shot before he makes his cynical reply, "Probably sleeping off a hangover. Why?"

The man reaches over to shake Joshua's hand. "I'm sorry, I haven't properly introduced myself. I'm John Stone. Would you like to join me for 18 holes?"

"I'll think about it. How's your game?" Then Joshua hits the last two balls in his bucket and rests on the top of his golf club while waiting for his new acquaintance's answer.

"Decent."

"By the way, I'm Joshua, and I guess I can meet you this Saturday, and you better be as good as you claim to be."

"Then it's a date!" exclaims John. "I'm hot and thirsty. Want to go for a beer?"

Joshua replies, "Sounds magical, but I cabbed over here from LAX and stopped here on my way home. Would you mind giving me a lift?"

John offers, "Not a problem. Where's your bags?'

After a couple of beers, the men are comfortable with one another. Joshua motions to the bartender to bring them another round. Joshua and John's shoulders are touching during their conversation, and Joshua notes that John didn't seem to mind it.

This man intrigues Joshua, and he wants to know everything he can out about him. "What do you do for work?" he asks.

John grabs a handful of peanuts from the bar and hesitates before eating them to answer. "I'm a pilot in the Air Force. What about you?"

"Engineer. I work for a NASA subcontractor at Northrop Grumman."

"That's cool. Are you hungry?" John inquires.

Joshua looks deep into John's eyes and replies, "Famished!'

After dinner John drives Joshua home and pulls up to the front door of his apartment building. He gets out of his car, walks over and opens the passenger door for him. John stands close to Joshua, almost touching him. He looks in his eyes for a sign that it was all right for him to kiss him. Joshua drank too much and misses his cue, so John steps back and says, "I had a nice time. Are we still on for

Saturday morning?" He says while handing him his suitcase and flight bag.

Joshua answers, "Positively. Do you want me to meet you at the golf course?"

John thinks about it for a second, looks up at Joshua's building and says, "I'd rather pick you up, plus I already know where you live. How's eight?" John reaches in his pocket for a pen and hands it to Joshua. Joshua writes his telephone number on a matchbook from the bar. Before giving it to John, he asks, "Can you come an hour early, so we can have a little breakfast before we go?"

John agrees, "Seven it is, and I like that idea."

#

Later that same evening, John enters his bedroom and begins to undress in the darkened room. His wife, Fanny, is already in bed and asleep. He accidentally bumps into a piece of furniture, and the noise wakes her.

Fanny speaks to him from the darkness, "John, where

have you been? I waited for you forever, and finally tossed your dinner in the trash bin."

John is a bit tipsy, so he answers her with slurred speech. "I thought I told you; I was going to the driving range tonight."

She pleads, "You did, but I expected you home by seven or eight."

He doesn't really care about the missed dinner with her and replies, "I ran into a friend on the driving range, and we grabbed a bite to eat."

His nonchalant tone makes her furious. "You could have at least called to let me know."

All he had to say for himself was, "I forgot."

Fanny rolls over with her back-facing John and pulls the covers up to her chin. John gets under the covers on his side of the king-sized bed and stretches out. Without saying goodnight, he faces away from her and begins snoring almost instantly. Fanny is so upset she cries herself to

sleep.

CHAPTER TWENTY-ONE

Penny is seated at her desk continuing to take notes on the telephone. It's an important message for Julie. She has on her eyeglasses when she reads the message back to make sure she jotted down all the important details. "The car will pick her up at her house at 5 a.m. There will be a car waiting for her at the airport in Houston, and it will take her to the MSC." She holds the phone in place with her chin while she finishes jotting down the last part of the dictation. "Yeah, I've got all the rest of it. Bye." After she puts the telephone back in its cradle, she massages the crook in her stiff neck and fluffs her flattened hair.

Penny gets up, pours a cup of black coffee for Julie and gently taps on her half-open door while holding the cup in her other hand. Julie is reviewing detailed plans of the Lunar Excursion Module and the Command Service Module. She writes down calculations on a scratch pad and is so absorbed in thought that she doesn't notice Penny standing there at first.

Julie has dark circles under her eyes; her makeup has rubbed off, and, from the look of her desk and clothes, it appears she spent the entire night working in her office. Penny wishes she could do more for Julie but feels helpless. She coughs to get her attention because the coffee is burning her hand. "Here's another cup of coffee. It's just the way you like it, black with two packages of saccharine."

Julie asks, "Did they call yet?"

Penny places the coffee in front of her, and grimaces as she replies, "Yes."

"And?" she queries with an anxiousness to her voice.

Penny squeezes her eyes shut before she reluctantly informs Julie, "They want to know if you fixed the problem yet." Julie has the look of horror on her face while Penny continues, "And they're sending a car for you."

Julie is panic-stricken, "When?"

"At 5."

This information makes Julie hysterical. She glances at her watch and inflects her already strained voice when she inquires, "Today?"

Penny immediately realizes her miscommunication. "Calm down. No, it's tomorrow morning."

Penny reads from her stenographer's pad. "Your flight to Houston is at 7:10 a.m. A courier is dropping off the airplane tickets this afternoon."

Julie begins pacing back and forth in her small office while thinking aloud, "I'll need every second to work on this problem. Penny, you must go to my house and pack a bag for me."

"Do you know for how many nights?" Penny begs.

"I don't and tell them to send the car to the office instead of my house."

"Okay" responds Penny as she jots down her instructions.

Julie raises her voice when it appears, she has an epiphany. "I need to call Debbie and make sure she can get the kids off to school for me again. Get Stanley on the phone!"

Penny runs back to her office, flips through her Rolodex, and begins to make the phone calls for Julie. She can feel her heart pounding in her chest over the urgency of the situation. It's an exhilarating feeling, and she is so proud to be a part of Julie's success on this project.

CHAPTER TWENTY-TWO

The black sedan picks Julie up at Houston airport and arrives at NASA's Manned Space Center. As it passes through the security gate, the guard notices she is asleep in the back seat. The driver shows him her official paperwork and puts his fingers to his lips as the sign for, "keep quiet." Julie sleeps through the entire security process.

From the driver's rearview mirror, she looks like a disheveled heap of wrinkled clothes, all curled up in a ball on his backseat. He turns around to look at her from the driver's seat and politely attempts to wake her. "Ma'am, we've arrived," he says gently as he pulls up to the main entrance.

She is dead to the world, so he sits there wondering what he should do about this perplexing situation. He turns on the car's emergency flashers, parks the car and sits. Then he pulls out his assignment sheet and is relieved to see that his next pickup isn't for two more hours. He places the sheet back under the seat and drums on the steering wheel deciding what to do next.

He turns off the engine and gets out of the sedan to smoke a cigarette. When he closes the car door, he notices her move a little; eventually she stretches her arms and yawns. It looks to him as if she might be falling back to sleep, so he crushes his cigarette on the pavement and rushes to open the back door to the sedan.

"Ma'am, we've arrived," he repeats in a louder and more authoritative voice. She gets out of the sedan and walks straight to the building like a zombie. She is adjusting to the bright sun, with blurred vision and the disorientation from being sleep-deprived, and she doesn't hear the driver say that he'll drop her luggage at her hotel. As she enters, all she has with her is her purse and briefcase.

When Julie arrives, she discovers no one in the Lunar Excursion Module Laboratory. She wonders for a moment if she might have wandered into the wrong room, so she goes outside to read the sign on the door one more time to confirm she is in the correct place. Then she looks at her watch and for an instant she thinks it might be 10 at night instead of in the morning. Once inside the MSC, determining the difference between night and day can be difficult. She looks around, and the large corridor is empty in both directions. Julie walks toward the cafeteria, and when she turns the corner, she notices a young man mopping the linoleum floor.

She asks, "Where is everybody?"

The man is happy to help and stops what he's doing. He says with a heavy Texan accent while pointing the way,

"Ma'am, I believe they're all in the auditorium."

Julie follows the arrows pointing the way and runs until she reaches her destination. She bursts into the crowed auditorium, and all their heads turn to look at her. It is a room full of men, as if it is understood it is exclusively meant just for them. Their surprised expressions suggests as if she had accidentally walked into the wrong bathroom and caught them peeing in the urinal instead of attending a seminar, because she is practically the only women in the room, she feels an irrational desire to apologize for invading their privacy. She searches back and forth desperately looking for an empty seat and realizes that the only ones left are in the last two rows. She sits down quickly while catching her breath.

A slender, attractive man in his 50's is speaking at the podium. There is a white movie screen behind him, and he is in the process of giving his lecture on NASA's upcoming plans.

Julie whispers to the man on her left, "Isn't that George Mueller?"

The man rudely ignores her question, but the man on her right who is too tall for his seat and sitting uncomfortably with his knees pressed up against the next row replies, "Yes, it is."

Julie boasts, "I used to work for him, and if NASA has a future, he's the man to lead us there." That's when she realizes the man she is whispering to is Sam Brown, the tall aerospace engineer wearing cowboy boots who she made eye contact with when she walked into the lab during her initial visit.

Sam quietly replies, "Thanks for the scoop."

Julie asks, "How much have I missed?"

"He just started," he comments casually. Then he looks at Julie's hand and notices she isn't wearing a wedding ring. He discreetly whispers in her ear, "I thought you were married."

His soft breath sends a shiver down her spine. She forces herself to speak even though she feels tongue-tied. "Not any longer, just finalized my divorce."

He grins as he says, "That's great, so's mine."

Julie's face flushes as she feels electricity coursing through her body. Sam Brown is not like anyone she has ever known, and he intrigues her. She wonders for a moment if he might even be an entirely different species from the men she has met up until then. It is almost impossible for her to focus on George Mueller's slide presentation about reusable fuel tanks for the upcoming space shuttle program. She's too distracted, and the only thing she can think about is what it would feel like to kiss Sam.

She looks straight ahead and tries to focus her mind from her wandering thoughts about what he might look like naked by listening to George Mueller speak in his clear and all-knowing voice: "Moments after liftoff, the space shuttle's emptied fuel tanks eject. They will be collected from the ocean and reused for the next launch." After that he clicks to the next slide which demonstrates the fuel tanks' retrieval.

Sam glances at Julie and grins again. She wonders if he had just read her mind and could hear her heart pounding in her chest. When the presentation is over, she hurries back to the Lunar Excursion Module Laboratory. She purposely loses track of him in the crowded corridor. It promises to be a grueling day flooded with seemingly unsolvable problems. As Julie wraps up the last of the day's many long meetings, she sits at the head of a conference table covered with plans, notes, calculations, full ashtrays, crumpled paper cups, and empty snack wrappers from the vending machine. Julie stretches and yawns before she declares, "I hope we fixed the glitch. We'll run the numbers on the computer, and it should give us the results by tomorrow night."

Then she collects her purse, briefcase, and wrinkled jacket. When she stands up, the room seems to spin around her, and she sways slightly. She admits, "I just realized that I have no way to get back to the hotel. Can one of you guys give me a lift?"

An engineer who had already reached the door turns back and asks her, "Where is it?"

"It's next to the airport."

He looks down at his shoes and says, "That's in the opposite direction from where I'm heading, and I'm trying to make it to my kids baseball game."

Sam is in the middle of packing up to leave, but he hesitates to see what her problem is and asks, "Julie, what's the matter?"

"No big deal. I was dropped off this morning, so I need someone to call a cab for me."

Sam swings his jacket over his shoulder and puts on his

cowboy hat. "Don't be ridiculous, you're coming along with me."

#

Sam drives a turquoise Ford truck. With a gentlemanly flourish, he opens the passenger door for Julie and walks around to the driver's side. Julie has no idea where he plans to take her and doesn't care. She feels comfortable with him and liked that he took charge. When he turns on the truck's ignition, loud country music plays on the AM radio. Sam ignores the music and rolls down his window to let out the heat that had built up over the hot, sunny day. Then he turns to her and asks, "So where are we heading, little mama?"

Julie confesses, "You know, I'm so tired I don't really know."

Sam sounds genuinely worried about her when he asks, "When was the last time you got any sleep?"

Julie thinks about his question before answering, "It was three nights ago maybe?"

"Where's your luggage?"

She laughs and slaps her knee. "I think I may have left it in the trunk of the car that picked me up at the airport this morning."

Sam is concerned for her welfare and continues questioning her. "Was that in LA or Houston?"

Julie is so confused and replies, "I'm not sure, but hope it's here."

Sam evaluates her situation and decides for her. "You're so overtired, you sound loco. I'm taking you back to my place where it's quiet, so you can get some rest."

Julie is embarrassed and argues, "Sam that's sweet of you, but it really isn't necessary." What's really running through her mind was how grimy and unpresentable she felt, plus she hadn't taken the time to shave her legs in almost a week.

Sam insists, "I won't take no for an answer." He peels out of the parking lot, leaving behind a trail of dust.

#

When Julie and Sam arrive at Sam's secluded ranch, Sam's hunting dog is waiting to greet them on the porch. Julie is sound asleep when he opens her door and wakes her. "Julie, we're here." He whispers softly. Julie's legs are wobbly, and she leans on him while going into the house.

Sam takes the liberty of unbuttoning Julie's blouse and removes her skirt and stockings. Julie cooperates and kicks off her shoes, as she climbs into his bed. All she has left on are her bra, panties and white slip. He pulls the covers over her and turns off the light on the night table. He quietly leaves the room and closes the bedroom door behind him.

He decides to sleep on the couch, even though there are other bedrooms in the house. Sam wants Julie to find him easily in case she wakes in the middle of the night and doesn't remember where she is. After tossing a pillow and blanket from the hall linen closet on the couch, he pours himself a beer, and carries it with a plate of food to the dining room table.

As he is eating his dinner, Julie peeks out from behind the bedroom door. She feels self-conscious because she is wearing only her underwear. She's partially hidden, exposing just her face, when she asks, "How long have I been asleep?" Sam looks at his watch, and estimates it was a little over two hours. She makes a simple request. "Do you have a robe I could borrow?"

He is more than happy to accommodate her. "Sure, it's hanging on the back of the bathroom door."

Julie quickly finds it, puts it on, and ties it tightly around her tiny waist. The sleeves are ridiculously long and hang practically down to her knees. She must take a moment to roll them up until she can finally see her hands.

Sam apologizes, "I'm sorry if I woke you."

"You didn't; it was the smell of frying onions. I must have been more hungry than tired."

Sam goes back into the kitchen and prepares Julie a plate of food and pours her a cold beer into a tall glass. He places the plate next to his and says, "Come join me and have something to eat."

Julie is thirsty and ravenously hungry. She devours the food and drinks with big gulps in between her large bites. It was the best-tasting steak she had ever eaten, and she loves the sweetness of the grilled onions and garden-fresh vegetables. After dinner, she feels much more relaxed with Sam. She looks around at his place and comments on the surroundings, "It's so quiet out here."

"I need to be away from everything," he explains.

Julie thinks that it's strange to live like a hermit, so she asks him, "Why's that?"

"I'm avoiding light pollution."

His answer confuses her. She'd never thought about it before and continues to question him. "I don't get it."

"Light Pollution." He states.

She had never heard of light pollution before, "What's that."

"It's easier for me to show you than tell you."

"Ok."

He downs the rest of his cold beer, and he gets up to open another bottle then poises it over her glass and waits for her response. She nods yes, and he pours it in her glass. Then he clarifies his reason for living in a desolate location. "I'm an astronomer, so if it ain't dark and clear, it's not worth my time."

Julie's feeling much better. She wants to let him know she appreciates everything he has done for her, so she collects the dirty dishes and offers to wash them. Right after she dries and stacks them, she confides, "I feel like a beast, may I use your shower?"

As Sam stands up and walks over to the kitchen sink, her eyes follow him. She still hasn't gotten over how tall and good-looking he is.

He turns and looks at her with his intense brown eyes and says, "Sure." He places the frying pan in the sink and runs some hot water into it to soak it. Just as she is about to enter the bedroom, he stops her and adds, "Wait right there a second." He returns in an instant with a clean towel for her that he retrieved from the linen closet and asks, "Do you need anything else?"

"I'd love a razor and some soap."

Julie feels refreshed after the shower. She combs out her wet hair, hangs up the bath towel, and then wraps herself in Sam's oversized robe.

She walks out of the bathroom and finds all the lights in the house off, and the front door is open. She crosses to the screen door and looks out to see Sam standing in the middle of an empty field, adjusting his large portable telescope in the dark. She quietly walks over to him. He is so engrossed while staring through his eyepiece that he doesn't realize she's there. "What are you looking at?" she asks.

He casually answers, "The Sea of Tranquility on the moon. Give your eyes a few minutes to adjust to the dark and come take a look for yourself."

Julie stands on her tiptoes to look through the eyepiece. For all the time she had spent sending someone to the moon, she had taken almost no time to look at it. She knew all the important scientific facts she used every day for her work about its mass, circumference, diameter, gravitational pull, albedo, average temperature, etcetera, but she had never seen it like this before.

Sam takes her by the hand to a couple of Adirondack chairs on his lawn. As they sit and look at the sky, Julie remarks, "Wow. There are so many stars up there. I never realized so many existed."

"Welcome to my planetarium. The show is about to begin."

"What show?" she asks.

"This is the time of year we get to enjoy the Leonid's meteor shower. The shower is much more impressive on a moonless night, but because the sky is so clear, we'll still have a spectacular show." They watch for a long time while they talk. Sam is curious and pries into her personal life, "What happened to your marriage?"

Julie is open to talking about it and shares some of her past with him. "We grew apart, but he's a great father to my three kids."

Sam seems surprised that she has so many children. "Wow, my ex and I never had any. That was really at the heart of the problem with our marriage. She hated kids, and in the end, she hated me too for wanting them when she didn't."

Julie awkwardly jokes, "Well, I can understand that."

Then she gasped and points at the meteor shower. "Look at that!"

But her comment confuses him and he's not sure if she meant it about not liking kids, so he asks, "Did you really mean that?"

Julie laughs to make light of her insensitivity. "Of course not! My kids are the best thing that ever happened to me."

"I hope to meet them someday."

"Who knows, maybe you will." Julie continues stargazing and asks, "So how did you end up working for NASA?"

"Same story as most guys here. I was a pilot in the Navy and flew enough hours to qualify for the early astronaut training program in, '59."

Julie is impressed. "That's so amazing! What happened?"

Somberly he reveals, "I didn't make it past the physical.

I'm just too tall, so I settled for second best. At least I get to talk to the guys up there." He points to the sky.

"How tall are you?"

Sam discloses, "6' 4" but 6' 6" with my boots on."

She's impressed and remarks, "You're 10 inches taller than I am."

"You know what that means."

"No, I don't," she nervously admits.

With a grin on his face he explains, "Well, if you can learn to fly a jet and pass the physical at NASA, then you can qualify to be an astronaut."

Julie likes his way of thinking but sarcastically adds, "Yeah right, an American female astronaut, like that will ever happen."

Sam takes her hand and says, "I think it's time for you to go back to bed, little mama."

When they stand up, he pulls her close to him, and she doesn't resist his tug. When they kiss, she realizes she had never felt the way she's feeling ever before. They barely know one another, but she wants to dispense with formality and rush head on into a sexual relationship with him. Their time together is so limited by the lives they live, and she understands they are too smart to play childish courtship games. In short, she rationalizes her desire to go to bed with him that night and decides it would be perfectly all right if she does.

Julie finds herself back in Sam's bedroom tugging at his cowboy boots in a frantic rush while Sam unbuttons his shirt and pulls off his pants. She drops his robe on the floor and leaps into his bed. He dives in after her.

Later that evening, Sam checks his glow-in-the-dark Timex and comments, "As much as I don't want to, I think we should get some sleep."

Julie rolls over and kisses Sam on the lips. This feeling of lust is new to her, and she's enjoying it. "Or maybe we should have another go at it."

In the morning after almost no sleep, Sam pads across the kitchen floor in his bare feet. All he is wearing are the pants he found in the pile of clothes on the bedroom floor. He fills his dog's bowl with dry food and makes a pot of coffee. He loves breakfast; it's his favorite meal of the day. He's whistling a tune while cracking eggs when Julie wanders in wearing his bathrobe.

She looks at the clock on the kitchen wall and exclaims, "It's 9:30! We've overslept, and we're late for work."

Sam places a huge bowl of water on the floor for his dog and stares incredulously at Julie. Then he asks her sweetly, "Darlin', do you know what day it is?"

Julie is still in a panic while she tries to figure out the answer. "No, not really, but my best guess is Friday."

Sam laughs before he says, "Relax, it's Saturday, and we're not getting the results from the computer for at least 10 more hours."

With a sexy tone to her voice Julie asserts, "Then I

guess we've got plenty of time." She walks up to Sam and embraces him. He takes her by the hand to his bedroom and shuts the door with his foot, so the dog doesn't follow them. The dog waits outside the bedroom door, scratches at it a couple of times, and then runs straight to the kitchen table to eat the bacon and eggs Sam left behind.

#

That night Julie and Sam drive back to the Lunar Excursion Module Laboratory to look over the computer results. Sam is excited, "It looks as if the LEM's descent problem is finally solved."

Julie agrees, "What a relief. I think we fixed the glitch, but they're not going to be happy when we tell them the wheels will have to come off the Lunar Excursion Module." Sam appears very upset at this revelation. She continues, "As badly as they wanted a billion-dollar golf-cart on the moon, it's not happening on this mission." She reads the results once again, but more carefully when she says with a smirk, "We'll have to start calling it just the Lunar Module." She shakes her head in disappointment. "Guess this is it for now. My work here is finished till it's built and delivered."

Sam sadly adds, "You know what that means."

Julie acknowledges his commentary and concludes, "I go back to LA."

Sam insists, "Julie, we can make this work."

"No, we can't, Sam. There are just too many obstacles."

"Name one."

She answers him defensively, "I can name four off the top of my head: my three kids, we live in different states, I might be a tad too old for you and we practice different religions."

Sam continues, "I can't leave my job until we land on the moon, and neither can you, but you'll be here more often as we get closer to launch."

She admits, "Okay, that's true, but I'm Jewish, Sam, and Jewish girls don't ride off into the sunset with handsome young cowboys."

"What if I became a Jewish cowboy?"

His comment stops her in her tracks, but she feels she must reply to it. She can see how sensitive he is about what he has proposed, and she doesn't want to hurt his seemingly vulnerable feelings. "I'll consider it." She replies.

Her last response is a relief to him. He reaches out, takes her in his arms, and hugs her. When she looks up at him with her brown eyes, she conceals her vastly conflicting emotions, and he kisses her. "You're different from all the other women I've known, and I don't want to lose you." He explains.

She believes he is speaking from his heart, but she also understands that relationships are complicated, and she can't seem to figure how this one could possibly work.

CHAPTER TWENTY-THREE

It is in the late spring of '69 when Joshua hears the
wonderful news that Julie and Sam are finally getting
married. He insists on making all the wedding
arrangements for them and happily steps into the role as
their planner. He enjoys living every moment vicariously
through Julie, as Joshua has always dreamed of being a
bride and longs to wear white, walk down the aisle, and be
the center of attention. He holds back nothing when it

comes time to decorate Julie's overgrown backyard, and even though she gives him carte blanche and never bothers to create a budget for him, he still manages to exceed it. He especially enjoys his research on how to make a proper Jewish wedding and figures out all the important details from books he picked up in the library. He wants everything about the wedding to be just perfect, and joyfully he discovers that going over the top is also an integral part of the Jewish tradition. Joshua even designs a customized yarmulke for Sam.

Since Sam's conversion to Judaism, he is more aware of the need for peace in the Middle East and in keeping with that, Joshua orders the yarmulke embroidered with two white doves.

Debbie is Julie's matron of honor, and she loves spending their special time together. It's as if it brought Debbie back to life and revived her from her long days of sadness. Julie can't figure out what's bothering her, but it has been years since she has seen that magic twinkle in her eyes.

Joshua is in the middle of bossing the caterer around with his right index finger, as he points out exactly where he wants everything placed, and he somehow manages to keep his left hand on his hip for the entire exercise. When he can't decide where he wants to put the enormous ice sculpture that depicts the launching of a Saturn Five rocket, he taps his forehead while thinking. He scans the yard until he locates the perfect spot and smiles when he makes his final decision. "Over there!" He pointes repeatedly and then rolls his hand with flourish to speed things up a bit.

Joshua adores the idea of a small tabernacle called a chuppah in Hebrew. It houses the bride and groom during the ceremony. Fresh flowers completely cover the structure, and he keeps returning to rearrange them to his liking while taking another whiff of their beautiful aroma. It's the first time he has ever seen a chuppah, and he's extremely proud of his magnificent creation. He knows everyone in the audience won't be able to keep their eyes off it. Then he chuckles at the thought of the shock on their faces when they get their first look at the bride.

In the audience from Julie's side are Julie's sister, Rose, and her husband, Penny and her three kids, Julie's parents, Yetta and Pop, Phil and his wife Stefanie, and Debbie's husband Joe. Julie's three children each have an important role in the service. David is Sam's best man, Matthew is the ring bearer, and Sara is the flower girl.

From Sam's side are his parents, his sister Laura, with her husband and their five ebullient children, and Sam's three brothers with their wives. It's far too busy back at work for any of Sam's or Julie's co-workers to take any time off, but they threw him a hell of a bachelor party in Houston before he left for LA.

Julie had a wonderful evening at the Tiki Hut with some girls from the office and a couple of her friends from the neighborhood. Penny and Debbie hosted it, and Julie was thrilled with the silly gag gifts they gave her. At any other time, she would have taken the gifts along on her honeymoon, but there wasn't any possibility of them getting away because the mission to the moon was coming up fast.

The guests are seated in the perfectly arranged folding chairs, and the rabbi is standing under the chuppah waiting for the procession to begin. Debbie cues the caterer to begin playing Pachelbel's Canon in D major from David's cassette recorder while Sam's mother and father escort him down the aisle. Sam is wearing a blue suit, striped tie and his new yarmulke. When they reach the rabbi, his parents take their seats.

Julie's mother and father escort her down the aisle. She follows behind Sara who drops yellow petals along the path. Julie spends more time dressing her children than herself and is worried that her dress isn't on straight. David has no idea how to tie his tie, and Matthew put on sneakers and white socks with his suit and insisted that it's "a look." She pleaded with him until the last minute, and he compromised with her by wearing his sandals after a lengthy discussion about today's fashion.

It's with Sara that she spends the most time. Sara had wanted to look like a fairy princess for the occasion. Julie set her daughter's long light-colored hair early that morning in big pink rollers and helped her into her chiffon dress. Julie was dismayed when Sara also argued with her over her choice of shoes. Sara wanted to walk barefoot down the aisle while singing the hit song, *Tiptoe through the Tulips*. When Julie asked her daughter where she got the idea, Sara shared that it was just something she felt she had to do. As it is a scorcher of a day and Julie is already at the beginning of her third trimester of pregnancy, she acquiesced to Sara's innocent request and allows her to skip barefoot down the aisle.

Julie looks ridiculous in her white lace, empire waistline wedding dress, and some people in the audience gasp as she passes by on her way to the altar. Her mother and father are proudly at her side and behave as if everything is as it is supposed to be. Julie takes her place next to Sam underneath the beautiful and fragrant chuppah. Julie's mother lifts the veil for her, and then her parents take their seats.

Except for the rabbi, the only other people standing are Julie's children, who remain for the entire ceremony. Julie whispers, so only Sam can hear, "I can't believe how long it took for you to convert! Look at me. Don't I look ridiculous in this dress?"

Sam softly speaks into Julie's ear, "I think you look beautiful."

After Julie marches seven times around Sam, they say their vows, and Sam breaks the wineglass with his foot. Julie looks back at the crowd and sees that both of Sam's parents are holding tissues up to their eyes, and they had cried throughout the entire ceremony.

As soon as the service ends, the caterer removes the folding chairs. Underneath the seats is the parquet dance floor, and the wedding ceremony is magically transformed into the reception. People get up to chat while they eat a variety of knishes and pigs in the blanket. A disc jockey plays dance music, until Sam's sister requests a square dance. Sam's father is the caller and happily instructs everyone how to do the dance. Julie's kids jump up from their table to join in the fun.

Julie is exhausted after the square dance and finds her seat. Phil joins her at the table. He endearingly places his hand on top of hers and says, "Look at you, you did it again."

Julie is curious and asks, "Are you referring to getting pregnant or married?"

"Pregnant. And I'm truly happy for you both."

"Thanks, Phil, but I can always tell when you're worried about something, so please tell me what it is."

He asks her, "When's your due date?"

"It's in the middle of the summer."

He seems concerned and reveals, "I just got the proposed launch date for the Apollo 11 mission."

"And?" she asks.

"What are the odds they are on the same day?"

Julie is now worried too. "From the look on your face, I'm guessing 30 to one."

Phil laughs and says "Pretty darn close, wouldn't you say? What's the worst case? If you had to of course you could always communicate with mission control from a phone in the delivery room, and they could relay your directions to the boys on the moon, right?"

Phil reaches across and gives Julie a kiss on the cheek before he states, "Congratulations, and I really mean it."

Then he gets up from the table, goes to the bar to get another double Chivas on the rocks.

Julie looks around at everyone having a good time and says aloud for her own amusement, "What a fun wedding. Now I need to go find my fairy god mother and thank him."

CHAPTER TWENTY-FOUR

Julie and Sam return to Houston right after the wedding.

There isn't enough time for them to go away on a

honeymoon because of its propinquity to the upcoming

moon mission. Julie is stopped at the gate before boarding

the flight and questioned about how far along she is with

her pregnancy, because the airlines has just instituted a new

policy that no longer permits pregnant women beyond the

eighth-month mark to fly. She must fast-talk her way onto the airplane and barely makes it on board.

As a wedding gift to them, Stanley steps in and helps Julie out with the kids. He's thrilled to have them for the month of July and makes plans for them to go fishing and camping on Mt. Rainier and hiking through the Cascade Pass.

#

Back at Sam's ranch, Julie is sitting in a rocking chair on the front porch. Sam had bought it for her as a wedding gift to nurse the baby on. Sam joins her outside and brings her a cup of chamomile tea. The waxing moon is almost full and so are Julie's tear filled her eyes. "Sam, I don't think I'll make it." She grumbles.

Sam is already grown accustomed to her pregnancy-induced emotional swings and tries to calm her. He knows whatever he says will be the wrong answer, but he tries his best. "There are some things that are more important than going to the moon, sweetheart."

His comment makes her instantly hysterical, and she reacts, "Not for me. I've worked too hard toward this one day, and it's been over the course of my entire life, and if there's anyone in the entire world who should understand how I feel right now, it's you!" She roars.

Sam gasps as he thinks, well that didn't go well, and he's too afraid to say anything else, so he decides to retreat and announces, "I'm going to call your mother and ask her to come. I think we're going to need her help sooner than we thought."

Julie rubs her enormous belly and sighs before she replies, "Thanks. If the baby arrives early, my mother can take care of it for us during the mission."

Sam can't believe she just said that about dumping their newborn child on her mother, so she can get back to work and runs off to make the call and not begin a big fight over where he thinks she should be.

#

The next morning, the security guard at the gate stops Julie and won't let her enter. "I'm so sorry, ma'am, but authorized friends and family enter at gate C." Then he points the way for her to go.

Julie erupts at the poor young man who is just trying to do his job, "You idiot, did you even look at my badge? I'm an engineer on the Apollo 11 mission." Terrified, he glances at the badge and opens the gate, even though there isn't even a scant resemblance between the woman in the ID photo and the woman driving the car that day.

Julie waddles across the gargantuan parking lot on her way to The Mission Operation's Control Room. When she finally reaches her destination, a confused man working at his console stands up from his chair to offer the seat to her. She motions no thank you and goes over to her appointed console, puts on her headphones, and taps on her microphone. Sam speaks to her through her headphones. "Good morning, Julie, you're late today."

For a moment, Julie forgets it's an open channel and replies, "From your lips to God's ears, I hope I'm very late!"

A chuckle travels throughout the room, and Julie realizes everybody has heard her last comment. Andy Kennedy walks over to Julie and squeezes her shoulder in an empathetic way. A few minutes later, everyone in Mission Control watches a textbook perfect liftoff of Apollo 11. The mission is displayed on the three screens facing the technicians and engineers. As soon as everything is calm, Julie waddles to the bathroom, Sam's eyes follow her out. When Julie returns, she gives him an okay sign, and she realizes how nervous he is, as this is his first but it's her fourth baby. She sits back at her console and focuses on her work.

Andy comes over to relieve her. "Go home. We don't need you until they reach lunar orbit, unless." She hesitates in the middle of the sentence.

Julie finishes it, "Unless something goes wrong."

"I've a good feeling about this mission. Get some rest." Andy insists.

Julie wants to kiss her to show her appreciation but decides it might look unprofessional, so all she says to her is, "Thanks."

Julie returns to Mission Control after her hiatus. It's when the Lunar Module and the Command Service Module begin the separation phase. She notices that her belly is lower and is worried that she might not make it through the day. Andy Kennedy is sitting at Julie's console while Julie stands next to her. They watch the maneuver, and both hold their breath until they hear back from the astronauts that it's a success. Andy turns to look at Julie and share in the celebratory moment with her, but her eyes notice something else, and she glances down. "Julie, look down on the floor." She commands.

An enormous puddle of water has formed at Julie's feet, and Julie says, "Oh, shit."

Andy jumps up, "I'll have someone from security drive you to the hospital."

Julie pleads, "Don't tell Sam, he can't be distracted right now."

Andy asks, "You sure?"

"Yes, I can do this without Sam." Then she points toward the viewing screen and states, "But they can't."

After what seems to be a terribly long ride to the nearest hospital, Julie finally arrives. She's fully dilated, and the baby is crowning. They roll Julie straight into the delivery room and almost simultaneously an orderly rushes in with a small portable black-and-white TV. Julie's first thought is they brought it into the delivery room to accommodate her, but quickly she realizes the nurses and doctors want to watch the lunar landing as badly as she does. No one pays any attention to Julie until after Buzz Aldrin announces, "The Eagle has landed," Julie bursts into tears of relief as the door to the Lunar Module opens on the moon. Everyone in the delivery room jumps up and down for joy. Eventually, the obstetrician in charge remembers he has a patient in labor and turns his attention back to Julie.

He snaps on his gloves and places his surgical mask over his mouth and nose right before he says, "Okay…" It appears he has spaced on her name, so he hesitates long enough to read her chart, and then he looks at her and repeats, "Okay, Julie, this is going to be a cake walk. Now it's time for you to push."

Only a few minutes later, Julie gives birth to her fourth child, and third son. Julie's eyes fill with tears of joy as she begs the doctor to show him to her, "Let me see the baby, please!"

Julie grabs the doctor's wrist, and he asks her, "What's the matter?"

Julie is panic-stricken when she inquires, "Is the baby okay?"

The doctor calmly replies, "Yes, he seems perfectly normal and healthy."

"Am I all right?"

The doctor chuckles and says, "So far, so good."

Julie sits ups on her right elbow and leans in toward the doctor, so they're eye to eye while she explains her circumstances. "You see, doctor, I need to get straight back to work. They need me at Mission Control for the ascent of the Lunar Module."

"Sure, they do, sweetheart. Here now… take a deep breath." The doctor places a mask over Julie's face and gives her a little gas to calm her down. As Julie slips into unconsciousness, she overhears the doctor instruct the nurse, "I want you to keep a close eye on this patient. She's either a lunatic, or she's having severe postpartum hallucinations."

"Yes, doctor," says the nurse, as she and an orderly roll Julie out of the delivery room and into recovery.

Later that night, Julie wakes feeling groggy from the gas. She looks around her hospital room while still dazed and confused. The curtain is half-drawn, but the first thing she notices is it's a private room. There are several flower arrangements haphazardly placed on extra bed trays scattered around the room. She props herself up and discovers a bassinet next to her bed. There's an oversized helium balloon depicting the moon's surface floating above the bassinet. When Julie reaches over to look inside the bassinet, she discovers it's empty and she panics. The television is on in the background and at that exact moment the Lunar Module is docking with the Command Service Module, which means the crew is preparing for their return to Earth. Julie ignores the TV and gets up to search for her baby. She pulls back the privacy curtain and finds Sam

standing there crying tears of joy while he is speaking

softly to his first-born child who is asleep in his arms. Julie

watches them spend their first moment together and

remains silent. A strange thought flashes through her mind.

She wonders if Sam is going to be as good a father as

Stanley had proven to be.

Sam doesn't realize Julie is awake when he asks his son,

"What's your name going to be, little man?"

Julie replies with a raspy voice, "I was thinking about

Isadore or Morris after my dead grandfathers." Sam makes

a face that demonstrates his displeasure with her

suggestions. Julie inquires, "What do you want to name

him? And I'm not even considering Buzz or Neil."

Sam can barely conceal his excitement as he reveals his

first choice. "I'd like to call him Max Q Brown."

Julie quickly responds, "I like that name, and it says a

lot about where he comes from. Plus, the M for Max works

with Morris as well. It's perfect!"

Sam proudly brags about his son, "There's something special about this kid; I think he's going places."

"Maybe he'll be the first Jewish president," Julie adds.

Without taking his eyes off his baby, Sam replies, "Or maybe even something better."

CHAPTER TWENTY-FIVE

Julie goes straight back to work after Max's delivery,

leaving him behind with her mother. Everyone in Mission

Control holds their breath during the blackout period while

the Apollo 11 capsule reenters Earth's atmosphere. When

the astronauts regain communication there are shouts of joy

and relief throughout the room. At that point, apart from the

recovery of the space capsule, the mission is successfully

completed. Julie tosses her headphones on the console and

goes to find Sam. He is at his console with his headphones resting on his shoulders.

Julie watches him from across the room for a moment. Sam is somber and silent. When she walks over to talk to him, she wonders what's bothering him. "Sam, what's with the long face?"

He replies without looking at her, "This is going to be a tough act to follow."

Julie is confused. She is supposed to be the one susceptible to postpartum depression and not the other way around. She squeezes his shoulder and inquires, "Why so gloomy at time like this?" Then she brushes his long brown hair back from his forehead and kisses him.

Sam confesses, "I'm overtired and starting to worry about my family's future."

An idea pops into Julie's head, and she says it aloud. "We need a vacation! I'm calling Stanley and telling him to send the kids down for the rest of the summer."

Sam likes this idea a lot and follows up with a suggestion, "How about we sail around the Gulf of Mexico?"

Julie smiles, "Sounds perfect."

"Great. I'll call my dad and ask him to find us a boat. But what about Max?" Sam's enthusiasm drains from his face."

Julie takes note of how emotionally fragile Sam has become and wonders if it is the fear of not knowing what to do now that his goal at work has been reached or something else. Then she happily explains, "Babies love boats; they rock back and forth."

Julie reaches for Sam's hand and asks, "Do you want to come with me?"

Sam stands up and tucks his shirt into his trousers. "Where are we going?"

"I want to go around and congratulate people on a job well done." Sam follows as she goes to find Phil. As soon as she sees him, she gives him a kiss on the cheek. He says

in her ear for only her to hear, "You're still my go-to girl."

After that she hugs Andy, and then places her arm

around her. That's when she spots Joshua from the corner

of her eye. He's sitting alone in the viewing gallery. She

runs up the stairs to speak with him and begs, "I want you

to come back with us to the house to see Max."

"I'd love to, but you must forgive me. I haven't had time

to buy him a gift yet."

"Max won't know the difference."

Joshua rubs his eyes and reveals, "Julie, I haven't taken

a vacation in five years. I didn't realize how tired I was

until the capsule splashed down in the ocean."

She takes his hand in hers and squeezes it when she

casually mentions, "Sam and I just said the same thing.

We're taking the children sailing. Where are you thinking

of going?"

Joshua whispers, "I'm thinking Provincetown. You know, on Cape Cod."

Julie can see that he feels uncomfortable and out of place at Mission Control, so she announces, "Let's all of us get the hell out of here."

Sam waits for Julie at the bottom of the staircase while he chats with Andy. He doesn't want to intrude on Julie's conversation with Joshua. Sam senses Joshua was experiencing something like his own feelings about achieving the goal of landing men on the moon. When Joshua and Julie descend the stairs, Sam initiates the conversation, "Joshua, why don't you join us at home for dinner? I'm barbequing and it's about time you meet the great, Max Q Brown." Julie is thrilled with Sam for being so keenly sensitive to Joshua and somehow knowing exactly what she wanted him to say.

CHAPTER TWENTY-SIX

The sailboat Sam's father selected for them is perfect in
every way and he got a great deal from one of his retired
navy friends who had contacts at the marina. There are
carved teak bunk beds for the kids, the main bedroom's
birth is enclosed on all sides, so they sleep with Max
between them. The big surprise for Julie is discovering
what a good sailor Sam is and how much he knows about
navigating around the Gulf of Mexico and great places to

stop and visit. Max loves the back-and-forth motion of the waves and never cries. His older siblings, David, Matthew, and Sara enjoy him so much that they never seem to put him down. Sara especially adores cuddling with him and begs to give him his bottles and helps with his bath. David endlessly watches his new brother's facial expressions change while he serenades him with his acoustic guitar. Often Sara joins in with her sax, Matthew pulls out either his harmonica or banjo. Everyone sings along, and even Sam has a nice voice.

For Julie the sailboat is the perfect remedy for her exhaustion from years of being overworked and under intense stress. There is virtually no housework, the baby's happy, and the kids live in their bathing suits, but the best part for her is Sam does most of the cooking. He enjoys grilling the fish he catches with the kids during the day. It's an easy-breezy time with lots of sun and happy smiles. She can't remember any other time in her life that made her feel happier, and it turns into the honeymoon she and Sam never had.

One clear night as the sun is slowly setting over the water in a gorgeous magenta blaze that fills the western sky over the open water, Sam pulls up to a secluded, white beach and moors the boat near the shore. Then he rummages around in the galley for a few minutes. Julie and the kids sit together and watch for him to emerge through the hatch. The kids laugh each time he bumps his head, as he continually forgets to duck. Sam comes back out and laughs when he says, "Thought I was going to whack my head again, didn't you?"

Sara giggles when she replies, "Yup, and what are you hiding behind your back?"

Sam reveals what was a carefully hidden bag of marshmallows and asks the kids, "Who wants to make a campfire on the beach and toast these.?" Then he shakes the bag over the kids' heads.

Matthew grabs his harmonica and a sweatshirt and climbs down into the dinghy. David hands his treasured guitar down to his younger brother and returns to the deck to lend a hand to his mother while she packs a few things for the baby and wraps him in a warm blanket. He reaches over to help her get into the dinghy while she carefully holds the baby and Mathew assists her as well. David makes sure she's seated in the center of the boat, and he double-checks that her life jacket is secure. Sam tosses down the bag of marshmallows and a box of safety matches to start the campfire. Sara balances the beach blanket over her arm when she crawls down the small, thin ladder and sits next to Matthew. David finds a spot between the guitar and his mother's back, and Sam sits across from Julie but has difficulty finding room for his long legs. The small outboard engine starts right up for him after one good pull, and it takes them less than a minute to reach the beach and pull the dinghy out of the water.

Sara and Matthew flip on flashlights and find piles of dried-out driftwood for the fire in the nearby woods, and David collects long thin sticks for everyone to roast their marshmallows. The horizon is turning to a burnt orange with flashes of pink. It's dusk and Julie watches the kids frantically running around collecting everything they need before the darkness arrives. She bounces Max in her arms to keep him contented. Sam stops working on the newly lit campfire and joins her by her side. They gaze at the last flickers of the sun setting over the horizon.

"Beautiful sight, isn't it?" Sam comments.

Julie agrees, "Yes, it is." Then she makes a happy and contented sigh.

Sam goes back to work on the building campfire and adds dry brushwood to it. The children return with enough twigs for everyone and sit by Julie and Max. David hands his mother a twig with a marshmallow poked onto the end, and she begins to toast it over the roaring fire, as Sam returns to roast his as well. She looks around, first at Sam,

and then at her children's happy faces. That is when she

realizes how blessed she is.

CHAPTER TWENTY-SEVEN

John's suitcase is butterflied open on the bed, and he is in the middle of packing while his wife, Fanny, badgers him. "Why, if you're going away for work, do you need to pack golf clothes?"

He grumpily repeats, "I already told you; I'm going to Hanscom Air Force Base in Massachusetts for some tactical training, and on the days off to Cape Cod for some golf."

Fanny's face reddens when she demands, "Why can't I come?"

He counters defensively, "No one's bringing their wife, that's why."

Fanny wonders if he is lying to her. She becomes hysterical and screeches, "You've robbed me, because you promised me, we'd have started a family by now!"

John places the last of the items on the bed into his suitcase and slams it shut before he protests, "We'll work on that when I return," but what he really means is that he'll say anything to just get out of the room without any further complaints from her.

She sneers at him and says with a smirk, "What a joke."

John usually knows better than to fall into one of her traps, but he just can't resist the temptation to say something and ask, "What's that supposed to mean?"

Fanny's face gets ugly when she regales, "Admit it, you're not even a real man."

John snaps when he thinks, that's it – I'm done. Then he grabs the suitcase from the bed and storms out of their bedroom without looking back.

#

It's almost impossible for John to put the memory of Fanny's mean face out of his mind. Joshua senses something is bothering him, and as they walk down the main drag in Provincetown, he confesses, "John, I want you to know that I love you."

It's a warm night in late August, and they're both too inebriated to remember he ever said it. The streets of Provincetown are bustling with homosexual couples sauntering arm in arm. It's like a New Orleans-style Mardi Gras celebration with dance music pulsating from the many bars and clubs. There are many more gay men than Joshua or John had expected to see. The men who surprise them the most are the ones dressed up to the nines as women in provocative and revealing clothing. Some of the men are so womanly that Joshua and John are fooled by them. As the night continues, the costumes become more elaborate. Joshua notices a man in assless chaps walk by and points him out to John, "Dude, check out Mr. Butt Cheeks."

John's eyes lock in on an exquisite version of Elizabeth Taylor dressed as Cleopatra, "Wow, she utterly gorgeous." He admits. At this point, Joshua and John have been drinking since breakfast and are propping each other up.

John drunkenly repeats to Joshua, "I love you more than anything."

Joshua echoes, "I love you too."

Joshua has a lucid moment and ask Joshua an infuriating question, "Why don't you divorce Fanny already and move in with me?"

As drunk as John is this question still strikes a nerve, so he ashamedly answers, "I've been thinking about it…" He turns away for a moment and looks up at the sky before continuing, "As soon as I retire from the Air Force and get a civilian job, I'll move forward with that."

Joshua is insensitive to John's feelings on this subject and has no idea that John is terribly upset about this subject when he adds, "Thank goodness there aren't any children involved."

John sadly confesses, "I've kept it that way on purpose. I truly feel she's someone who should never have kids."

Joshua asks while slurring the words, "Why, don't you like kids?"

"Of course, I like kids. It's because she's such a mean, cold-hearted bitch."

Joshua is so drunk he can't walk without hanging on to John for support. "Then why did you marry her?" he inquires.

John's body stiffens while he explains, "If I hadn't, I never would have moved up in the ranks. The Air Force isn't kind to guys like us."

"I'm sorry, that was a stupid question. I often forget because of Julie."

John immediately worries that Joshua might have left some personal details out about his past and jealously asks, "What about Julie?"

Joshua boasts about his female friend, "Oh, she's just the most amazing woman ever to walk the earth besides my mother." At this point, John is becoming upset, but Joshua is unaware and continues anyway. "For example, a couple of years ago, she pretends to have an interoffice affair with me just to get the gorillas off my back."

Joshua's explanation appeases John's sudden burst of distrust, and he comments, "That was awfully gallant of her."

Joshua carries on, "I can't wait for you two to finally meet." Then he catches himself from falling right before he declares, "I love you both so much."

John reaches over and places Joshua's arm over his shoulder. He realizes that Joshua is too far gone to walk back to the hotel on his own, so he suggests, "I think it's time to call it a night."

Joshua winks at him and says, "Sure thing." And then he stumbles before he says, "I love this place."

CHAPTER TWENTY-EIGHT

1974

Julie is in the middle of rearranging the furniture in her large corner office. She wonders if she should also move one of the sofas to the other side of the room where there is a better view from her floor-to-ceiling window. She looks up at the framed portrait of President Nixon and says under her breath, "It's time for you to go." Then she replaces it with a poster of Golda Meier. The caption on it reads, "But Can She Type?" Julie steps back to look at the poster on the wall and chuckles at the joke. She holds Richard Nixon in her hand for a moment while she tries to decide what to do with him and then unceremoniously drops him behind the small sofa in the corner.

Penny announces to Julie on her intercom, "Phil's here to see you."

Julie talks to herself some more when she looks up at the ceiling and asks, "Shit, what's he doing here?" Then she walks back to her desk and nervously replies over the intercom, "Send him in." Julie sits down under the poster of Golda and waits for him.

Phil enters and firmly closes the door behind him, takes a seat and crosses his legs. He looks around and notices the changes to the surroundings. "I see our old commander and chief is gone from the wall, so did you vote for Nixon?"

She replies smugly, "Do you know anyone who didn't vote for Nixon?"

Phil shrugs before conceding, "I guess you've got me on that one."

"Phil, what's this visit about?"

"Straight to the point, is it? I'm here to discuss executive order 11246."

To appear innocent, she asks, "What about it?"

Phil nervously reaches for his pack of cigarettes, takes one out, and offers her one.

"No thanks, I still don't smoke."

He lights it, and inhales.

His uncharacteristic stalling tactics frightens Julie. "You're not here to fire me, are you, Phil?"

Phil smirks as he ignores her question and bitterly continues, "That would be pretty hard for me to do as you're practically a legend around here from your team finding the extra power needed in the lunar module to bring the boys back on the failed Apollo 13 mission."

"That wasn't just me."

Phil seems exasperated with her, "I'm sure this isn't just you either. I get how all the women from the typing pool, craft services, and the switchboard wanted to come to your little pow wows, but how did you get all those broads from the assembly plant to sign your stupid antidiscrimination petition?"

Julie respectfully explains, "I let each one of them know how much money a man who does exactly the same job is getting paid."

What she's saying upsets Phil as he sternly demands, "How the hell did you get your hands on that information?"

Julie swallows before she lies, "I've no idea where it came from, Phil."

He bangs his hand down hard when he says, "Cut the crap, Julie."

"One morning I found a manila envelope slipped under my office door. It listed the different job levels performed by men and women and it documented the discrepancies in salaries."

Phil is visibly peeved. "I really don't want to know how you got it, do I?"

Julie stands up as she inquires, "So, are you are here to escort me out of the building?"

"No, not at all. Please sit back down."

Julie is relieved and sinks into her seat. The thought of Mathew's orthodontics bill, David's new band equipment she promised him, Sara's summer camp tuition and the big backyard renovation that Sam is working on flash through her mind as she feels relief over dodging this bullet, "This isn't about just me, is it?"

"Nope, it isn't!" Phil grinds out his cigarette in her clean, crystal ashtray that's really an empty candy bowl that she was just about to fill, "Word about the data leak has gotten around the office, and upper management wants to meet with you."

Julie informs him, "Tell them I'm ready." Her stomach twists into knots and she can feel her heart racing from fear, but she doesn't regret what she did.

"I hope you understand this puts you in the front and center of this situation when the cannon balls go off."

Julie says decisively, "It's worth it to me, Phil."

"For your sake, I hope you're right." He gets up and walks out of her office.

As Phil heads straight back to his office, he passes Florence but doesn't even glance at her because he's fuming over the data breach, and he has his suspicions as to who would work in cahoots with Julie. He slams his door shut and dials an extension on his telephone. "Fanny!" He stammers, "You were supposed to be gathering useful information for us at those meetings." Phil lights another cigarette while he listens to her excuses. Then he angrily shouts, "What the hell did we pay you to do then?" Phil slams the telephone down, grinds out his cigarette into his full ashtray, and shakes his head in utter frustration. Not only is he worried about his own career but some of the people he cares the most about at work are also on the firing block along with him. He ponders, oh Julie and Florence what have you done to us?

#

Later that week, Penny sits next to Julie at a large table in the busy cafeteria. Julie is wearing her eyeglasses and reading a memo while several other women join them: Susie, Linda, Florence, Fanny, and Jean come in from the main building, and Beverly, an older woman in a jumpsuit and with her hair in a net, has just arrived from the assembly plant. They sit down and wait for Julie to start the meeting officially.

Julie announces, "Let me call this meeting to order. Penny, please take note of our attendance for the minutes." Penny checks off the names in her roll book."

Julie looks around the table with a stern expression. "I

have some news to share with everyone."

Before Julie can speak, Fanny interrupts her, "Jean, Linda, Florence, Susie, and I have something to say."

Julie shrugs off the interruption and says, "The floor recognizes, Fanny."

"We want you to remove our names from the petition."

Julie unapologetically states, "It's too late."

Fanny is outraged by her reply, "Look what you've done, Julie! Where going to lose our jobs over this and Susie's husband is out of work, Florence's husband recently passed away, and the rest of us are scared to death we'll be fired if we go any further with this."

"You don't understand." Julie tries to explain, but before she can finish her sentence, Fanny, Jean, Linda, and Susie stand up from the table and start to walk out.

Julie raises her voice and pleads, "Wait!"

Fanny sneers at Julie with contempt, as she continues to walk away. Julie decides it's best to ignore her and continues the meeting. Jean, Linda, and Susie are halfway between Fanny and her.

Julie turns to Florence and says softly, "Thank you, Florence, for staying." She leans over and whispers in Florence's ear, "And for the data list from personnel."

Julie winks at Florence, and Florence smiles back before she explains, "After my boy died in Vietnam, I began to see things more clearly, especially, when it comes to understanding the difference between what's right and what's wrong." Florence confidently folds her hands and takes a deep breath.

Julie stands on her chair to make the announcement because she wants everyone to hear her, not only the people at her table, but all the men too. "We did it!" She broadcasts while clinking her fork on her empty glass. "As of today, we, the women employees of Northrop Grumman, are getting paid the same salary as the men!" Cheering erupts around the room from some of the men and almost all the women, many of the women hug and clap in celebration of one another. Some of the men in the room look terrified by her announcement and remain silent.

Simultaneously, Linda, Jean, and Susie stop at the door and turn back to join in the revelry, but Fanny huffs out of frustration and storms out of the cafeteria. Everyone else is congratulating Julie for her hard work.

#

Later that night, Julie places a bottle of champagne she bought on the way home on the kitchen counter and takes out two fluted glasses. She notices the kitchen is messier than usual, but she's in such a good mood it doesn't bother her. She decides to look in on Max first and finds him already asleep in his bed. The house is quiet, so she kicks off her shoes, and goes outside to the backyard to find Sam. She carries the glasses between her fingers in her right hand and the bottle of champagne in the other. Sam's relaxing in their brand-new hot tub with a couple of the overly friendly new neighbors. The women are topless, and the men are drinking beers. She discovers one of the men passed out and Sam seems to be flirting with his young wife.

The women were handing a joint back and forth when Julie urgently asks, "What's wrong with him?" Pointing at the unconscious man.

The young, bleached blond elucidates, "Chill, he took a Quaalude."

Sam ignores the dialogue and asks Julie, "What's the champagne for?"

Julie smiles and says, "A celebration."

"What are we celebrating?" He's concerned for an instant that he might have forgotten their wedding anniversary.

Julie states proudly, "I got a raise today." Then she pops the bottle open and hands out the two glasses, one to Sam, and the other one to the blond sitting next to him.

"Woo Hoo!" she exclaims.

Julie returns with a few more glasses and passes them around to the rest of her strange new neighbors that she doesn't particularly care for and is trying to figure out how to get them to leave.

Meanwhile, Sam holds up his glass and makes a toast, "To my amazing wife, Julie. Every other engineer in America is out of work and looking for a job, but no, not her! Instead, they give her a raise today."

His comment feels like a slap in the face, and she says, "Cut it out, Sam. You don't have to be sarcastic."

Sam looks down at the hot bubbling water. "Sorry, being out of work is making me nuts." He drains his glass in one gulp and holds it up for her to a refill right after he asks her, "Why don't you join us."

Julie returns in a flash wearing her faded one-piece bathing suit. She gets into the hot water and cuddles up near to Sam, not because she wants to be close to him but instead to push the topless girl he's flirting with away. She reaches for her glass of champagne and takes a tiny sip. The other topless girl who remained quiet up until that moment begins to make out with the bleached blond girl. Julie gives Sam a look to say she's feeling uncomfortable, but the two girls kissing each other has mesmerized Sam, and he ignores Julie.

After the neighbors leave, Sam and Julie get ready for bed and turn down the bedspread together. Julie demands, "Why didn't you stop them when I asked you?"

"First of all, I never heard you, I swear." he reacts.

She tosses a pillow at him, "You're such an asshole."

Sam asks, "Why are you being so uptight, and what's the big deal about two women wanting to get it on?"

She defends her feelings about the situation. "I wasn't raised that way."

Sam finishes his beer before commenting, "No one was, but I was pretty turned on by it."

She's intrigued, "Really?"

He grabs her and talks like a caveman, "Woman come here."

She giggles from the thrill, but implores, "Quiet, don't wake Max."

He makes soft grunts, and she laughs when she asks him, "Are we all right?"

He ignores her question and instead, he pulls her into his arms, and they roll into the bed together.

CHAPTER TWENTY-NINE

Debbie dumps a basket of clean laundry on her bed and begins to fold the clothes while she chats with Julie. Meanwhile, Max plays in the background and makes an appearance every so often. He loves Debbie and often stops whatever he's in the middle of doing to flirt with her.

Debbie is confused when Julie tells her about what happened in the hot tub the night before and doesn't understand why she's upset when she asks her about it, "I don't know what the hell you're complaining about. You've had more sex in a week than we've had in all the years we've been married, so why are you angry with Sam? I don't think he did anything wrong."

Julie ignores Debbie's criticism and focuses on her comment about her lack of sex. "So, why don't you say something to Joe about your needs?"

Debbie sticks her fingers down her throat and pretends to vomit. "Truthfully, I prefer it this way. I'd rather a bad case of crabs than sex with that slob."

Julie is puzzled. "Why don't you divorce him?"

"I can't because of money." Then she moves over the pile of folded towels to make room for the rest of the unfolded clothes on her bed.

Julie can't believe how helpless she seems and makes her an offer in earnest. "Debbie, I'll help you out, and Joe will have to ante up and pay you alimony."

Debbie states sternly, "You don't understand, and it's way too complicated to explain."

Julie is insulted. "I'm not a birdbrain, you know. I'm sure if you speak slowly enough, I'll..."

Debbie interrupts, "I've never shared what I'm about to tell you."

Julie sits down on the bed in anticipation of this big reveal. "Now you're frightening me."

Debbie grasps a handful of clothes up to her chest and says while looking up at the ceiling, "I don't want to pay that asshole any of my hard-earned money."

Just then Max pops out from under Debbie's bed and asks, "Who's an asshole?"

Debbie says apologetically, "Oh, my God. I didn't mean say that in front of Max."

Julie calms her down, "Don't worry, it's not the first time he's heard that word."

Debbie continues, "I spoke with a divorce lawyer, and

he explained that I'll have to fork over half of what I've saved to Joe."

Julie throws one of the decorative pillows at Debbie before she says, "You goofball, I almost believed you!"

Debbie grins and returns to folding the rest of the clean clothes. Just then Max jumps out from Debbie's closet holding a huge pink vibrator that's humming away in the tight tiny grasp of his little hand. Max screeches with elation, "Look, Mommy, I found a laser."

Debbie immediately turns beet red from embarrassment and pleads, "Oh, my God, Max, give that to me!"

Max shouts, "No, it's mine, I found it." He holds the loud vibrator over his head, as Debbie chases Max down the hallway. Debbie eventually trades a large, homemade hot fudge sundae with a cherry on top in exchange for her pink vibrator. Julie can't remember seeing anything funnier in her life than watching Debbie negotiate with Max that day.

#

After Julie and Max go home, Debbie leaves for the post office where she has rented a mailbox. She opens it and takes out a single envelope. Then she walks across the street to the coffee shop and takes a seat in the back corner of the last booth at the end. She looks around first and then opens the envelope. Her eyes glance straight down to the statement's summary on the first page. It lists her stocks, and the number of shares she owns. The list includes Coca Cola, Budweiser, Procter and Gamble, Clairol, Disney, Esso, Wal-Mart, MacDonald's, IBM and many other successful corporations. Debbie takes the last sip of her coffee and places the statement in her purse. As she gets up to leave, she drops a quarter on the table for the waitress. After that she heads straight home, opens the oven, places the statement inside, closes the oven door, and sets it to self-clean.

CHAPTER THIRTY

Julie and Max are eating their breakfast together in silence at the kitchen table. Julie's eyes are following the new housekeeper as she washes the dishes, and Max's eyes are watching his mother watch the housekeeper. Julie hasn't fully recovered yet from losing Maria, her trusted housekeeper and nanny of over 18 years. Maria didn't want to leave the family but had to move home to take care of her ailing aging mother. This housekeeper is a young and perky Hispanic woman. But, as much as Julie wants this new person to work out, there's something about her that just doesn't seem right. When she puts away the last coffee cup, Julie mentions, "Make sure you get caught up on the laundry because my kids are coming home this weekend."

The housekeeper smiles and says, "I'll start right away." Then she leaves the room and goes to separate the colors of the dirty clothes and towels.

Julie turns to Max and asks, "How would you like me to drive you to school?"

Max cheerfully replies, "Goody! I want the top down."

Julie's new bronze Mustang convertible is in the driveway. It only takes her a few seconds to unlatch the top and follow Max's request. Max sits next to her with his window rolled down. His arm extends out the window with his little starfish shaped hand slicing through the air as they drive along. Julie passes the neighborhood gas station/convenience store, and the sign out front reads,

"Empty." Then she passes another station she and Sam never go to because the gas is higher priced and discovers a line of at least 25 cars waiting to fill up their tanks. She checks her own gas gauge and is relieved to see it reads three-quarters of a tank.

When they reach Max's new alternative elementary school, he gives Julie a peck on the cheek, hops out of the car, and enthusiastically runs up the front steps. She's glad she and Sam decided to send him here instead of the local elementary school where he was bored witless. Max waves to his mother right before he enters the big double doors. She wonders if she should have parked her car and walked him to his classroom, and a little voice in her head tells her to stop hovering over him.

It's a beautiful, clear morning, and Julie can already tell it's going to be a hot day. Along the way to work, Julie notices more stations are out of gas. She passes one off the highway with a line of at least 50 cars. Then there are cars stranded on both sides of the road because they ran out of gas while waiting in the long line. As she approaches the office, she notices Penny walking to work on the shoulder of the busy road. Julie pulls over and hollers at her, "What the hell are you doing out here? It feels like it's already 90 degrees. Get in."

Penny sits in the car and closes the passenger door. Julie resumes her drive to work. Penny doesn't explain her circumstances but exclaims, "My lord, that fan feels good on my face!" Penny lifts her blouse to allow the cool air under it. Then she asks Julie, "Do you happen to have a gas can?"

Julie answers, "On me? No, why?"

Penny describes her circumstances in detail. "I ran out of gas about two miles back, and the service station wants 50 bucks for an empty gas can."

"I think I've got one in the garage that used to belong to Stanley."

Penny smiles before she comments, "Ah, Stanley. I still love that man."

Julie agrees, "Me, too."

Julie pulls up to the front of the office building, drops Penny off, and parks the car in an almost empty garage.

When Julie gets to her desk, Penny has placed the day's newspaper and a cup of black coffee on it for her. Julie reads the news with trepidation, as each headline is worse than the one before it: OPEC, recession, Arab oil embargo, runaway inflation, rising unemployment rate, rising interest rates. It's clear to her the balance of power has tipped, and the oil-producing countries are gaining control of the world's economic destiny.

She shudders at the thought of being under the thumb of the OPEC nations, which include seven Arab countries, which are now in charge of the new world order, and she worries about the fate of Israel, a tiny, democracy the size of Rhode Island struggling against these antisemitic

Goliaths. How will Israel ever survive the pressure from this reign of terror?

Penny interrupts Julie's nightmare scenario by talking to her on the intercom, "Joshua's here to see you."

Joshua barges in and begins to pace back and forth. Julie looks up at him for an explanation and is astounded when he blurts, "Well, it's official; you're my only friend who still has a job."

Julie gasps, "What are you going to do?"

Joshua collapses into the chair across from her and says, "Collect unemployment and live off my retirement savings until I find another job. What else can I do?"

"Please let me help you out."

Joshua replies in a solemn tone, "No thanks. And you should hold onto your shekels because who knows? You may be the next to go."

At this Julie stands up and begins to pace. Then she looks at him and says, "I think I'm going to scream."

Joshua runs his fingers nervously through his hair and says, "Well, I've already found a silver lining."

"How can you be so upbeat at a time like this?" she wonders.

He explains, "Things aren't all bad. John decided this is the perfect time to tell his wife he wants a divorce."

"Why now?"

Joshua replies with a smile, "He's a laid-off commercial pilot. Between the two of them, she's making more bread than he is, so she can't sue him for alimony."

"I didn't realize how badly the oil embargo is effecting the airlines." She admits.

"America is one giant empty gas tank, with no jobs, no flights, no industry." Joshua reveals.

Julie brings their conversation back to the subject at hand and asks, "But seriously, what are you really going to do?"

Joshua sounds defeated when he responds, "Not a

clue." Then he adds with a contemptuous smirk. "You know all the money I made over the years?"

She acknowledges cautiously, "Yeah."

"Well, I spent it on clothes, booze, and boys. What do you think of that?"

Julie loves Joshua with all her heart and searches for something to console him and assuage his anxiety. "At least it made you happy."

Her comment makes him grin, and he agrees, "Yes it did." He glances down at her desk and notices she wasn't working on anything. "I'm going to the nearest bar to get blitzed. Do you want to join me?"

"You sure you want me to?" She knows Joshua doesn't like to have her around him after he has had a couple of drinks.

He insists, "I would love your company and I don't want to be alone right now, plus your buying."

Joshua reaches out for Julie's hand and escorts her by

the arm. When they open the door, Penny looks very nervous. Julie is worried there's more bad news and asks, "Penny, what's the matter?"

"You left your intercom on, and I heard the entire conversation. Do you think I'm next?"

Julie is always one to speak the truth and says, "Who knows? So, would you like to come along with us?"

Penny packs her oversized purse while answering, "Well, my car's out of gas, and there's nothing left to work on here." She tucks her chair under her desk and pushes the night service button on her telephone. "Let's go."

CHAPTER THIRTY-ONE

It was an awful morning at the office and an even worse afternoon calming Penny down while trying to keep Joshua from drinking himself to death. On her way into her house, Julie nonchalantly waves to Joe who is also just getting home from the office. She predicts Sam has already consumed a couple of beers over the course of the afternoon and will be in an ornery mood. Long-term unemployment has wreaked havoc on him, and she doesn't know how much longer he will be able to take it.

She decides to avoid conflict with Sam and instead goes to search in the garage for a gas can to bring to Penny. She closes the garage door behind her because she doesn't feel like chatting with anyone, especially not Joe.

Joe watches Julie's garage door close and is grateful that he does not have to make small talk with her because he just had one of the lousiest days in his life, if not the all-time lousiest. He stands at his front door, as if it were the precipice of a steep cliff and takes a deep breath before he enters.

Debbie is tossing a salad and drinking white wine. Joe can tell from the bottle that it isn't her first glass and he's happy about that. He's as white as a ghost, and his lips are clenched together. He walks straight to the bar while trying to think what he's going to say, as he pours himself a stiff drink. He takes a gulp trying to gather his courage and sits down at the kitchen table.

Debbie is startled by the way he looks and asks, "Joe, what happened? You seem upset."

"I had a terrible day, that's all." Tears fill his eyes as he says, "Debbie, you're the best wife any man could ever dream about."

Debbie is concerned and dread floods her mind. She prepares herself for him to tell her he has a fatal illness when she asks him again, "Joe, what's the matter?"

"I did something really stupid, and I don't know how to tell you."

That's when her thoughts flash to Colleen's message on the answering machine about her paycheck bouncing. Joe has had a long history of covering up his gambling debt problem, but now with money being so tight it's probably finally caught up to him.

Debbie is frustrated and urges him on, "Joe, you're upsetting me. Tell me what's going on."

"Why don't you pour yourself another drink and sit down over here."

Debbie tops of her glass of white wine and joins Joe at the kitchen table.

Joe is ringing his hands and his knuckles have turned white as ash. "I need to come clean and confess everything to you."

"Go ahead, I'm listening."

He says, "I had an affair with my secretary."

Debbie is about to say something, but Joe cuts her off and adds, "That's not the worst part. The bitch was a con artist." Joe pulls out his lighter and watches for her reaction, then lights a cigarette. He composes himself before he continues, "Who was I kidding? Why would a young, attractive woman want anything to do with a fat, balding, old fart like me?"

Debbie is merciful and comments, "You're not that old." Meanwhile, her bull shit detectors are going off in her head.

He hits the table and yells, "Stop being so nice! You're making this harder for me than it already is."

Debbie sees right through it. He doesn't want her to be nice or feel sorry for him and she tries a different tack, "All right, Joe."

Something in Joe just snaps, and now he's obviously reciting memorized lines, "That bitch cleaned me out and took my last stinking dime. She emptied every single one of my savings accounts."

Debbie says in a stern voice, "Don't you mean our accounts, Joe?"

Her correcting him brings him back to reality, and he agrees, "Yes, of course, our accounts."

Debbie notices that his glass is empty and goes to get the bottle of scotch from the bar. She asks while holding the bottle above his glass, "Would you like a refill?"

"Yes, please." Then he stares down at his shoes like he's searching for the next words to say.

Debbie pours scotch in his glass and Joe's hands tremble while he lights a cigarette without realizing he has one already burning. He inhales deeply before he continues, "The only thing she couldn't get her filthy hands on was the cash value to my life insurance policy because you're listed as the owner."

Debbie is not particularly concerned with Joe's measly finances. In fact, she is disappointed that he doesn't have some life-threatening illness, now that she steps back and thinks about it. She's officially done, it's over, and she doesn't have an ounce of pity for him, so she decides to change the subject and asks, "Joe, what about your poker game tonight?"

"As soon as I found out what Colleen did to me, I cancelled it."

In an almost mechanical way she inquires, "Would you like some dinner?"

"Maybe, later. I'm not hungry right now." Joe looks like a zombie when he turns to her and comments, "Debbie, you're taking this awfully well."

Debbie must quickly conjure a satisfactory response, so not to arouse Joe's suspicion and replies, "I think it's the shock." She walks over to the sink, puts on her pink rubber gloves, and robotically washes the dirty glasses.

#

Across the street at Julie's house, the housekeeper has just cleared Max's dinner dishes from the kitchen table. Julie watches the body language between the young, attractive girl and Sam. She is wearing green rubber gloves while she submerges the greasy plates into a sink full of hot sudsy water and smiles at Sam at the same time. Sam reaches into the refrigerator and takes out another beer and smiles back at her from over the refrigerator door. Seeing this upsets

Julie, but she doesn't mention anything about it and attends to Max who asks sweetly, "Mommy, come read me a story."

She looks at the two of them with consternation and then raises her voice to say, "Max, I'll be right there." But neither of them notices her.

As Julie and Sam are getting ready for bed that night, she wonders how she's ever going to fall asleep. She has the financial weight of the entire family on her shoulders, while the world around her is coming apart at the seams. Sam gets into bed first and begins to read a book. Julie gets under the covers and right after she makes herself comfortable, Sam's hunting dog stretches across her legs at the end of the bed. Julie is heating up from the dog and pushes the big guy off her with her foot and sits straight up before she announces, "Sam, we need to talk about the housekeeper." Sam appears startled and she isn't sure if it's because he has a guilty conscience or the of her alarming tone of voice.

"What about her?" he asks coyly.

Julie reveals in an accusatory way, "I think she took something from me."

Sam doesn't seem to believe her. "Oh, really? What's missing?"

Julie doesn't appreciate the way he comes to her rescue and says in a huff, "Go to sleep, we'll talk about it another time, but I'm placing an ad in the paper first thing in the morning and then I'm firing her."

Sam adds calmly, "Isn't that a bit rash?"

Julie defends her decision, "I don't think so."

Sam reaches to touch Julie on the shoulder but hesitates. He has the good sense to know when she's too irritated for a calming touch, and he backs off before he comments, "I can tell that something else has upset you."

Julie instructs, "I don't want to talk about it, go to sleep." She pulls the covers up to her nose and turns her back to him, so he leans over and whispers in her ear. "You'll sleep better if you tell me what's bothering you." Then he closes his book and waits for her to say something.

She barks back at him, "You, you're bothering me!" Julie can't stop what happens next. Her eyes fill with tears as she begins to cry into her hands. Sam reaches over to peel them off her face. "Julie, I know you like a book. Something terrible has happened, and you're blaming me."

Julie is so confused by the events of the day that she babbles, "I'm not blaming you, damn it, and why do we need a housekeeper anyway? You're home all day long doing nothing!"

Her comment cuts into him deeply and hurts his feelings. She knew that he was going to job interviews and using the time to set up meetings and send out his resume.

"For Christ's sake, what the hell has gotten into you tonight?" he hollers.

Julie burst into inconsolable tears and is making no sense. After she catches her breath from crying, she feels more relieved, "Joshua was fired this morning!"

Sam attempts to console her. "That's just awful. I feel for the guy and know what he's going through."

Julie turns to him and says, "It's only a matter of time until it's me. What are we going to do?"

Sam puts his arms around her and confesses, "I didn't want to get your hopes up, so I've been saving the news about my upcoming job interview."

Julie wipes away her tears with the bed sheet and says, "Really?"

"Don't jinx it!" He begs.

The good news helps her to calm down. "Okay, no more questions." She submits.

He offers in a reassuring and trustworthy voice. "Try not to worry. I'm sure Joshua will land on his feet." Then Sam kisses her on the top of her head and pats her gently.

"There there, try and get some sleep."

PART THREE

CHAPTER THIRTY-TWO

It's the morning after Joe confessed to Debbie about his alleged affair with his secretary. He feels too ashamed to face her. The night before he had a couple of drinks before heading home, but the thought of confronting her sober terrifies him. He pretends to be asleep, and as soon as she leaves the bedroom, he runs straight into the master bathroom and closes the door behind him. His stomach is inside out from nerves and before he knows it, he's throwing up into the toilet.

Debbie prepares breakfast for Joe like usual and plugs in the percolator for a pot of coffee. She pours herself a fresh cup, sits down at the kitchen table, and thinks about how miserable her marriage is to him and decides the cost of a divorce will be worth it in the end. She sips it slowly because it's too hot to drink at first. The house is silent apart from the shower running in the master bathroom. Suddenly, she hears a loud thump, and it makes her accidentally spill some of the hot coffee. Debbie blots it up with her napkin. The noise is so loud that her first thought is a large branch must have fallen from one of the older trees in the backyard. She has already been through enough this morning and has no interest in investigating and discovering a new problem. She decides whatever it is, it can wait. She continues to sip her coffee while thinking about the upsetting things Joe told her the night before.

After she finishes the coffee, it occurs to her that the shower has been running for a long time. She touches his breakfast which is now cold, and thinks what a waste, before she ventures out to see what's been keeping Joe.

When she enters her bedroom, she discovers water pooling under the master bathroom door. She opens the bathroom door and finds Joe lying on the pink and gray tile floor. Draped over his body is the shower curtain, and the pole is on top of him because when he fell, he took everything down with him. The water from the shower is spilling over onto the floor, so Debbie climbs over Joe's body to turn it off.

Joe can't move a muscle, and he struggles to say, "Debbie, I think I'm having a heart attack."

Debby stoically glares at him.

He says with difficulty, "I made up the affair with Colleen." Debbie backs up and looks at him. Joe uses up almost all the strength he has left to plead, "Help me."

Debbie thinks about how unhappy she has been and for so many years, she has nothing to say to him. He makes one more attempt in vain to communicate with her and says, "Dial 911." Then he gasps for air and passes out.

Debbie exits the bathroom and closes the door behind her. She quickly pulls on a pair of shorts, a blouse, and a pair of sandals. She nervously removes the pink rollers from her hair and places them on top of the bedroom dresser. Then she thinks about making the bed and decides not to. Instead, she walks outside to get some fresh air. That's when the idea pops into her head; she should stick to her normal routine. It's a typical Wednesday morning, so she loads a couple of crates of empty bottles and cans in the rear of her old, rusted station wagon just like usual, only she barely has any because Joe cancelled his poker game the night before. Julie sees her and pulls into Debbie's driveway. Her convertible top is down, and Debbie stops what she is doing and goes over to talk to her.

"Morning, Julie. Where are you off to so early?"

"I need gas. I'm down to an eighth of a tank, and the line isn't too long if you get there before 7."

Debbie nonchalantly remarks, "You're always the clever one."

"I'll be back right after that to drive Max to school."

As if it's like any other day Debbie asks, "Do you want me to give Max his breakfast for you?"

Julie sounds relieved when she says, "That would be great." Then she points toward her garage and opens it with the remote control while adding. "By the way, there are six more crates of empties. Do you want them?"

Debbie is stone-faced as she casually mentions, "Joe cancelled his poker game last night, so I've got plenty of extra room."

Julie is in a rush and is already backing out of the driveway when she replies, "Thanks."

Debbie waves to Julie as she drives off and then walks over to Julie's house to get Max. She brings him back to her kitchen and serves him a fresh new breakfast, while ignoring Joe's cold plate of eggs and bacon. She pours milk into Max's bowl of Rice Crispies, then slices a banana and places the pieces on top of the cereal. While Max is chewing, she asks, "Max, would you like a Pop Tart?" Max has a mouthful of food, and he enthusiastically nods yes to her offer. Debbie rips open a package of Pop Tarts with her teeth and inserts one in the toaster. Then she makes what seems to be an innocent comment, "I better go and see what's taking Joe so long."

Max replies with a mouthful of food, "Okay."

Debbie exits the kitchen and returns in the blink of an eye. She puts the Pop Tart on a plate and places it next to Max's bowl of cereal. "Would you like a glass of milk to go with your Pop Tart?"

He glances up at her with his big brown eyes and replies

politely, "Yes, please."

Debbie fills a glass with milk, places it next to the Pop Tart, walks across the kitchen, picks up the handset on the wall telephone, and calmly dials 911. Max watches her while he chews his Pop Tart.

Debbie speaks clearly and calmly into the receiver, "Can you please send an ambulance?" Then she gives the dispatcher her address and describes the exterior of the house before she adds, "I think my husband's having a heart attack."

Max springs off his chair to go look for Joe in the other room. Debbie drops the telephone. It bangs against the wall, as she grabs Max by the waist to stop him from running to see Joe. At that moment, Julie returns from getting gas and takes Max from Debbie's arms. She picks up her hysterical son and holds him in her arms while she asks, "What's going on?"

Debbie calmly explains, "I just called 911. I found Joe unconscious on the bathroom floor."

Julie has the strongest desire to flee that house. She has the eerie feeling from the tone in Debbie's voice that Joe is already dead. Julie has never seen a dead person before and feels uncomfortable, especially since it is someone so young and she knows so well. She tugs Max's hand and says, "Let's wait for the ambulance outside so we're not in their way."

Joe is toes-up on a stretcher with the sheet over his head when he is rolled down the driveway and into the quiet ambulance, as the sirens are off and the people on the emergency medical team are no longer rushing around. Julie has her arm around Debbie and is firmly holding onto Max's hand because he wants to look inside the ambulance and watch what is going on. Sam notices the commotion and joins them. As they stand all together in the street, they watch the ambulance back up and drive away.

Max asks, "Where are they taking Uncle Joe?" No one bothers to answer his question.

Sam is dazed and addresses Julie, "Did you get gas?"

"Yes," She replies.

Sam stretches out his hand, "Give me the keys to the Mustang, I'm taking Max to school."

Julie is also in a daze. "Okay," she mutters and hands him the keys.

Sam realizes Julie is in shock, so he speaks resolutely to Julie, "Why don't you take Debbie inside? I'll be right back."

Julie puts her arm around Debbie and guides her to her kitchen. Debbie walks over to the wall telephone, picks up the dangling handset, hesitates to collect herself, and then dials a number she knows by heart. Julie sits down at the table and watches her in silence.

Debbie struggles with her words. "Marilyn, Joe just had a heart attack." Debbie listens for a moment before she replies. "Yes, it was fatal." Without shedding a single tear, she adds. "I can't believe it either." She takes a deep breath and looks up at the kitchen ceiling while listening to Marilyn. "Yes, I'm all right," is the last thing she says before she hangs up and starts to cry.

Julie says sympathetically, "Why don't you go lie down while I clean up the mess."

"Okay," Then Debbie makes her way to her bedroom. Julie collects a mop, bucket, and pair of pink rubber gloves.

When Julie enters the bedroom, Debbie is lying on top of the unmade bed. Julie doesn't know what to say to her, and she walks straight into the master bathroom. She drops down the mop and bucket and puts on the pink rubber gloves. Meanwhile, Marilyn has entered the bedroom and is unaware that Julie is in the bathroom.

Marylyn cries out to Debbie. "Sweetheart, we can finally be together." Debbie quickly reacts. She puts her right index finger to her lips and points to the bathroom. It is too late; Julie hears what she said and emerges from the bathroom holding a large green sponge.

Julie is confused by Marylyn's comment and while trying to figure out what is going on, introduces herself, "Hi, I'm Julie, Debbie's neighbor." She removes the pink rubber gloves and extends her hand to Marilyn for a handshake.

Marilyn looks at Debbie for a cue, and Debbie nods that everything is all right.

Then she proceeds to introduce herself, "Hi, I'm Marilyn, Debbie's girlfriend."

Julie stammers, "Excuse me?"

Debbie can tell from Julie's expression that she is completely perplexed, so she offers an explanation. "Marilyn and I have been seeing each other for a long time. I just didn't know how to tell you." Marilyn kisses Debbie on the top of her head to comfort her and sits down next to her on the bed. Debbie continues, "We were afraid Joe might find out about us and about the money."

Julie eyes open wide when she says, "You mean that cockamamie story was true?"

Debbie grins, "Yes, and the first thing I'm going to do with Joe's measly life insurance policy is blow it on a fancy new sports car."

Sam returns from dropping Max at school and enters the bedroom. He nonchalantly waves hello to Marilyn as if he already knows her. Julie catches it but chooses to ignore it. Instead, she asks, "How was Max when you dropped him off?"

Sam replies, "Pretty upset."

Julie has second thoughts about sending Max to school, "Maybe we should have kept him home today."

Sam utters, "Yah, maybe you're probably right." Then he turns his attention to Debbie and reaches to take her hand in his and says, "I'm so sorry for your loss."

"Thanks Sam, you've been a good friend to Joe." Then she changes the subject, as if she doesn't want to talk about him any longer and asks, "Does anyone want some coffee, I can put up a fresh pot?"

Sam replies to Debbie, "Stay, I'll get it for you. Please, don't get up." He turns to Julie, "Want me call Penny and let her know you're not coming in today?"

Julie gasps before she says, "Oh, my goodness! I forgot all about her. Her car ran out of gas, and she abandoned it on the side of the road. I'm supposed to bring her a gas can."

"Did you remember to fill it?" he asks.

"Yes, and it's in my trunk."

Sam bends down and kisses her on the forehead before he volunteers. "I'll take care of her for you. You should stay here with Debbie."

Julie is upset with herself for forgetting. She looks up at Sam and says, "Thanks. I'll stay and help her with the funeral arrangements." Sam kisses her goodbye and is off to rescue Penny.

#

Later that morning, Julie enters the kitchen to answer the telephone which is ringing non-stop. She is in the middle of a conversation with the undertaker when Stanley walks in and sits down. The dirty dishes from Max's breakfast still clutter the table.

Julie says to the person on the telephone, "Thank you for answering my questions. Goodbye." She waves to Stanley and puts up her finger to let him know she'd be off in a minute. Right after she hangs up the telephone, she sits down across from Stanley at the table.

"How is she holding up?" he asks.

"Surprisingly well," Julie remarks.

Stanley shakes his head from side to side. "I can't believe Joe's dead."

Julie agrees with him. "It doesn't seem real to me either."

Stanley asks endearingly, "So how are things with you?"

She decides to be honest with him about her situation. "I'm worried about my job."

He reaches across the messy table and places his hand over hers. "Julie, I'll always be there for the mother of my children, and you know how much I adore Max as well."

Tears form in Julie's eyes. She has a connection with Stanley that she doesn't have with Sam. Stanley always knew how to make her feel safe and secure. "I want you to know something." She stops talking for a moment to wipe the tears away and collect her thoughts. "I married you for all the wrong reasons."

Stanley moans, "Please, we've gone over that a thousand times."

"Let me finish," she adds. "What you don't know is I also divorced you for the wrong reasons. I've come to realize that you're the finest and most decent person I've ever known."

Her compliment catches him off guard. He doesn't know how to respond to it, so he changes the subject, as he squeezes her hand. "We raised a nice bunch of kids."

Julie confirms, "Yes, we did."

CHAPTER THIRTY-THREE

A year has passed since Joe died from a heart attack. Sam

has transformed into the family's breadwinner, and Julie's

position as the project manager and aerospace engineer at

Northop Grumman ended with a generous severance

package. Sam is dressing for work, and Julie is under the

covers relishing the idea that she isn't in a rush to get to the

office in traffic.

She looks at him and admits. "I like this."

Sam asks her while tying his shoelaces. "What, sleeping in again?"

"Yeah, and I really like collecting unemployment."

"You earned it every penny of it." He leans over to kiss her goodbye, "I'm still impressed how many years you held onto your job."

She feels slightly guilty and asks, "Do you want a ride to the airport?"

"No, I'm all set, got a ride. Enjoy yourself, read a book, or do some gardening."

Julie makes a simple request. "Send Andy my love."

"You sure you don't want to come along with me to Houston?"

"I'm sure, Sam. I need to be here for Debbie and take Sara shopping for school clothes." Julie gets up and stretches to reach Sam's lips to give him another kiss.

#

Later that morning, Julie saunters in between Debbie's

Porsche 911 convertible with racing stripes and Marilyn's

large Mercedes sedan on her way to their front door. She

stops to admire the aerodynamics of the sports car and runs

her hand over its spoiler. Julie knocks lightly on the door

and enters without waiting for a response. She makes her

way into the kitchen and when she can't find anyone

hollers. "Morning, ladies, are you up yet?" Then, she pours

herself a cup of coffee from the percolator.

Debbie waddles barefoot from her bedroom wearing a

brightly colored maternity dress. She's in her third

trimester of pregnancy. Marilyn follows right behind her

with a pair of fluffy slippers and bends down to put them

on Debbie's feet. "Here you go. Don't forget these."

Debbie sounds apologetic. "I need to pee, but I'll be

right back."

There is an uncomfortable moment between Marilyn

and Julie while Debbie is out of the room. They can hear

Debbie humming while she pees with the bathroom door left wide open. Julie can't think of anything to say to Marilyn and feels awkward.

Right after Joe died Sam explained to Julie why he didn't tell her about Marilyn. He believed that Marilyn and Debbie's unconventional relationship would take Julie some getting used to, and he didn't want to jeopardize the closeness between her and Debbie. It was inevitable that he found out about their affair because he was home all day while he was looking for work. Julie still finds being alone with Marilyn uncomfortable, as she hasn't figured out what their relationship is supposed to be.

Eventually, Debbie flushes the toilet and announces, "I could go for some Chinese."

Marilyn hunts in the refrigerator and finds a white container from the previous evening's leftovers. Debbie eats right out of the carton with her fingers. "Oh, my, I think it's better the second day."

Marilyn rubs Debbie's huge belly, as Debbie boasts, "I still can't believe it only took one insemination and voila." Her comment confirms Julie's suspicions as to the identity of the sperm donor, but she decides it's none of her business and she doesn't inquire but has no doubt it came from Stanely.

Debbie looks over at Julie and asks, "Now that you're a lady of leisure, what do you plan on doing today?"

Julie replies, "I'm meeting Joshua and John for lunch. We're celebrating the finalization of John's divorce." Julie glances down at her watch and realizes how late it is. "I've got to get going." Then she offers, "On my way back I'm stopping at the market. Do you need anything?"

Marilyn replies, "No thanks, we're all set. I've been stocking up for the big day."

#

Joshua's ultramodern office building and lobby astounds Julie, and she's truly impressed with its over the top lavishness. There is obviously an enormous difference between the decorating budgets for a low-bidding government defense subcontractor and a profitable Fortune 500 corporation. She sits quietly across from Joshua while she waits for him to end his business call. She enjoys being near him because it feels comfortable and familiar. Despite their relationship being way past the point of making small talk, she feels nervous in the new surroundings.

"How's the job?" she asks as an icebreaker.

He admits with flourish, "I just love it here."

She knows how much he enjoys talking about himself and she indulges him. "What do you do exactly?"

"The company makes commercial aircraft, and my department designs the interiors. My favorites are private orders. OMG so decadent."

She also knows how to get a rise out of her old friend and adds, "Nice, but I like a challenge."

Joshua scowls when he admits, "I don't miss the space

race."

"That ended when we launched the Apollo-Soyuz joint mission."

Joshua retorts, "The rat race never ends. Speaking of which, how's Sam's new job?" he asks with a smirk.

She is almost too embarrassed to confess and takes a deep breath before she replies, "It's his old job, only harder, and with longer hours, oh and for a lot less money."

Joshua knew that there would never be another Apollo mission and wondered, "What's he doing now?"

The thought flashes through her mind about what Sam really is, an old dog training the new dogs how to do better tricks, but instead she replies, "Training the next generation at Mission Control for the shuttle."

Joshua can't resist. "Ah, the world's first space age aerodynamic moving van."

Julie defends the value of Sam's job. "It's a good project, and it will take him to his retirement."

Joshua changes the topic because he has the sense to know they're not getting off to a good start, and he really misses her companionship. "How's married life?" he inquires.

"Not without its aches and pains. Being the wife of a tall, handsome man, who is eight years younger, has its challenges."

Joshua is pleased she is being honest with him and replies, "It's the same for us. Lots of work, and the whole monogamy thing is a pretty new concept for me."

Just then there is a light tap at the door, and John enters the office. He looks especially handsome in his airline pilot's uniform. Joshua and Julie stand up to join him and leave for lunch. Joshua proclaims, "You two are going to love our cafeteria. It's right out of *2001: A Space Odyssey.*"

When Julie arrives home after lunch, Sara informs her that Debbie went into labor, and she wants Julie to be with her in the delivery room. Julie jumps back in her car and goes straight to the hospital. It's difficult at first explaining to the woman at the desk why Julie belongs in the delivery room along with Marilyn who is already in there. The woman at the desk wants to know where the baby's father is and why he isn't attending to his wife. Julie gives up trying to explain the situation to her and goes to find Debbie on her own.

Debbie and Marilyn give birth to a beautiful, healthy baby girl, Julie devotes most of her spare time to helping them. Debbie doesn't have a clue how to take care of a newborn baby, and Marilyn is worse than useless.

Julie often wondered what had happened to Debbie's mother and why she'd never met her. After Lilith's birth she discovers the truth, Debbie's mother had abandoned her and her father when she was a small child. That must be the reason she never mentioned her. Julie realizes that Debbie has no one else to call for help besides Marylin, and after the numerous times Debbie came to her rescue, she's happy to reciprocate.

Sam begs Julie to spend more time with him in Houston, so she promises him that as soon as Max is away at summer camp, she'll join him. Lilith is just beginning to sleep through the night, and Julie believes it's a good time to let Debbie know she needs to go away for a while to be with Sam.

#

It's her first trip back to Houston in a long time. She and Sam fly down together. They're both wearing their bifocals to read and are working quietly. Sam has the shuttle's electrical diagrams in front of him when he comments, "I'm so glad you joined me. Here, look over these schematics."

Julie confesses, "I'd love to."

Sam passes them to her, then gets up to go to the lavatory. The lavatory is occupied, and he waits for it while

an attractive female flight attendant appears to recognize
him and flirts. Julie notices it right away and calls to mind
the flight attendant Joshua hooked up with back in their
early days at NASA. Julie watches Sam over her bifocals,
as he appears to look around to make sure Julie is still in
her seat and the coast is clear, and then it seems he decides
it would be harmless to flirt back with the young woman
and he does in plain sight. Just then, Julie stands up to get
something from the overhead compartment, and she peers
over at them chatting. She takes a pen from her carry-on
and slams the overhead compartment shut to get his
attention, but he's so enamored with her he doesn't even
notice. Eventually he uses the lavatory, and on his way
back to his seat the young and attractive stewardess slips
him a small piece of paper which he slyly slips into his
pants pocket. Julie doesn't say anything about what she
thinks she saw. Her only comments are about the

schematics he left for her to enjoy, but she's fuming hot

inside and pretty sure she gave him her telephone number.

CHAPTER THIRTY-FOUR

The next day Julie and Sam rise early at their ranch on the outskirts of Houston and decide to head straight to work. While Sam is in the shower she goes through the pockets of his pants from the day before and finds a note with a phone number on it. She wants to strangle him and doesn't know what she should do about the situation. She tries to clear her mind. She consoles herself that it might be meaningless, and she shouldn't jump to any foredrawn conclusions. When he tells her he's out of the bathroom she remains silent and keeps her thoughts to herself.

#

NASA had changed the Manned Space Center 's name to the Johnson Space Center in 1973, but everything else is pretty much the same and Andy Kennedy manages to keep her job throughout the economic ups and downs of space exploration. Julie believes that Andy could very well be the person responsible for turning off the lights if the place ever does close for good.

Sam has a staff meeting coming up and suggests they get something to eat for breakfast. Andy is expecting Julie and is looking across the busy cafeteria for her. She spies Julie at a table with Sam, waves to get her attention, and comes straight over to them. Sam kisses Julie goodbye and leaves while chewing his half-eaten bagel, after he says a polite hello when Andy arrives. He appreciates these two old friends haven't seen one another in a while, and they have much to discuss. Additionally, there are rumors floating around that Andy's forty-year marriage is crumbling.

Andy recollects how much Julie hated the Russians, so she greets her using an outrageous Russian accent. "My old comrade, what are you doing here?"

Julie giggles at the silliness of Andy's accent, but much appreciates that she remembered how she felt about their space race. She answers Andy's question in a straightforward manner and says, "Max went to overnight camp for the summer, so voila, where here and everything is wonderful."

Andy's eyes unexpectedly flood with tears. Julie briefly wonders if it's because she's so happy to see her, or if she has some dreadful news to share. Andy clarifies things rather quickly when she asks, "Did you hear the gossip about me?"

"No, Sam doesn't repeat much. Andy, what's going

on?" She's genuinely worried for her friend and holds her breath while waiting for her to reply.

Andy tries to control her emotions. "My husband left me for a much younger woman and started a new family with her. He's a sixty-five-year-old man for god's sake."

Julie gasps and doesn't know what to say. "I'm so sorry for you." That was the only thing she could think of at that moment.

Andy describes while trying to catch her breath, and my kids are flabbergasted. When their father inherited money from his folks after they passed, it never occurred to any of us that a gold digger would go after him. My daughter won't talk to him anymore, and she doesn't want anything to do with him or his new kid. His little chickee is just a year older than our son. It's simply insane."

"Oh my god." Is all Julie can say. Then she recalls how there was so much trash talk around their department when she married Sam because he's eight years younger than her, but this is an entire other kettle of fish compared to her situation and then she feels a shiver run down her spine.

Andy looks down before she states. "I feel as if I stepped on a land mine."

Julie asks, "What are you going to do?"

Andy looks around the cafeteria and acknowledges, "I'm ready for a change, and this place isn't as much fun as it used to be. Just look over there." Andy points to a troop of about 50 Girl Scouts on a guided tour. "Can you guess where they're camping tonight?"

Julie admits, "No idea."

Andy scoffs. "The Apollo mission control room."

Julie is amazed. "Isn't MOCR a restricted area?"

"Not anymore. NASA turned it into an interactive exhibit for kids."

This upsets Julie. "That's shocking."

Andy continues, "The part of my job that I hate most is

the weekly reports. They want to know the number of paid visitors and the gross sales of the gift shop.

Julie commiserates with her, "That's just awful."

Andy announces loudly, "I'm done! Let someone else decide which snack food is the biggest seller and what is our top grossing ice cream flavor on the tour." Then she lowers her voice when she asks Julie, "Do you want my job?"

Julie tries not to insult her with her reply, "No, it's too administrative for me, and all I ever wanted to be is an engineer."

Andy confirms, "I had feeling you'd say that, but it kills me to see you wasting your talent."

Julie assures her. "I'm not! When I get back to LA, I'm interviewing for a great job."

"Please have them call me regarding your references. After what you did to help save those boys on Apollo 13, it's the least I can do." Then something across the room gets Andy's attention. "Hey, look over there." Andy points to a table of four women wearing flight suits. "All of them are astronauts in training, and they think they're too good for the rest of us."

Julie huffs before she comments, "It only took them 20 years for NASA to catch up to the Russians with regard to woman in the space program."

Andy is indignant. "Those women have no idea how easy they have it. We didn't just pave the road for them, we bulldozed down the trees and cleared the way."

Julie asks, "And who paved it for us?"

Andy smiles before she enthusiastically bangs her hand on the table and speaks. "Nobody! We were the pioneers."

Andy's pager beeps. She looks at it and remarks mockingly. "Oh shit, there's a crisis in the gift shop, must run. It was so nice seeing you, Julie."

Julie agrees and adds, "Same here."

CHAPTER THIRTY-FIVE

Julie's new office is larger and more luxurious than her previous one. It's futuristically decorated in a nihilistic way – as in form over function. She is the project manager for her department, and the wall that separates her office from the main area is made of clear glass. This allows her to look out and watch what the other engineers and their secretaries are doing. After all the hanky-panky that happened where she used to work, she appreciates the transparency.

Hanging on the interior wall above the sofa is a large portrait of President Ronald Reagan that was placed there by the company's interior decorator. There's one just like it in every project manager's office to constantly remind everyone who they work for. On her desk are the work-in-progress schematics for the Hubble Space Telescope and a desktop computer.

Julie's new secretary, Cathy, interrupts her thoughts when she buzzes her on the intercom to inform her that her 10:00 a.m. appointment has arrived.

"Please send her in."

Julie watches Fanny Stone walk towards her. Julie has no idea why she called to request a meeting with her. They never liked each other very much, and Fanny had stabbed Julie in the back whenever she found an opportunity. Still, they grew up together in Brooklyn, and the least Julie can do is hear her out. So, when Fanny faces her, Julie gestures and says, "Have a seat." Julie moves some papers around as she looks across at Fanny's wrinkled, tired face. A strange thought crosses Julie's mind as she wonders if she has aged as badly as Fanny.

Julie doesn't have spare time to play games, so she gets straight to the point. "What can I do for you, Fanny?"

"First, I want to tell you how sorry I am for the horrible things I did to you over the years." Julie is startled and doesn't know what to say, so Fanny looks Julie in the eye and continues her confession. "I was such a bitch to you." She swallows and twists her fingers together. "It was because I just couldn't control my jealousy of you."

Julie is puzzled. "You were jealous of me? Why?" Julie is truly dumfounded. She thinks about how they grew up together in the same poor neighborhood in Brooklyn and besides Julie's ability to keep a job, they're not that different from each other.

Fanny tries to explain herself, "You made everything look so easy when it was actually very hard for the rest of us."

If Fanny's objective is to throw Julie completely off balance and catch her by surprise, then she's succeeded. Julie doesn't know what to offer other than an apology. "I'm sorry for doing that to you," Which were the last words she ever imagined herself saying to the evil and mean-spirited Fanny Stone.

Fanny asks, "Why are you apologizing to me, when I was the one who repeatedly tried to make your life miserable?"

Julie nervously laughs, "Just can't help it, I suppose."

Fanny proceeds to reveal the real reason why she came to see her. "Look at me, Julie. I did everything I was told to do, and now I'm middle-aged, divorced, and without a job."

Julie tries to make Fanny feel a bit better about her

situation. "It's not entirely your fault. The economy is terrible right now."

Fanny seems encouraged by Julie's rationalization of her financial situation. The comment makes her feel a bit more at ease, so she asks. "Do you remember that stupid guidance counselor we had back in high school?"

"Sure, I do. She was horrible."

Fanny continued, "Did she tell you to skip college and go to charm school like me?"

"Yes, wasn't she a dope. I've no idea how she got her job."

Fanny asks, "Did you hear she was eventually fired years later for hitting on a teenage girl?"

"It figures. So, what can I do for you?" Julie doesn't mind reminiscing, but she is positive that Fanny came to see her for more than that.

Fanny sets aside what is left of her pride and speaks up,
"I need a job."

"I don't ..."

Fanny interrupts, "Julie, after John left me, I went back
to school and got my bachelor's degree at USC."

"Congratulations, that's big accomplishment and it's
where I received for my master's degree."

"Thank you. I want you to know, I'm no longer a
frightened, naive girl who thinks a prince will come along
and rescue me. I've changed, and I owe it to you."

Julie doesn't know how Fanny's comment is supposed
to make her feel. Seeing Fanny in such a bad place in her
life doesn't bring Julie any joy, and she's way past wanting
to get even with Betty Ann Abramowitz and Fanny Gold
for trying to make her miserable in high school. Julie found
her niche, and she ended up enjoying her big group of
friends as much as the next kid. Early on, she accepted the
fact that she was going to do things differently and made

the best of it. Most important, she knows there is no right or wrong way, as people need to do what works for them.

Julie is being sincere. "I've only been here a couple of months, but I'll see if there's anything available and get back to you." Julie has nothing more to say and stands up, so Fanny understands their meeting is over.

Fanny appears grateful. "Thank you for seeing me. By the way, I went back to using my maiden name."

"Gold, wasn't it?" Julie confirms.

"Yes, that's right. Well, I guess you're real busy," replies Fanny, as she gets up from her seat.

Julie nods yes, so Fanny leaves her office, and Julie takes her seat. Fanny appears disappointed and forlorn as she passes the model of the Hubble Space Telescope on display in the waiting area and finds her way out of the building. She stops at the front door and turns around to look at the building, as her heart fills with regret.

Eventually Julie's secretary enters, places some mail on Julie's desk, and a folded over *Los Angeles Times*. She doesn't want to disturb Julie while she's concentrating, so she returns to her desk on the other side of the glass wall without uttering a word.

Julie glances at the newspaper, but what catches her eye is an ominous looking thick manila envelope on top of the pile of mail. She reads the names on the return address. It's from a law firm that she's never heard of, and she wonders what this is about. She carefully unfolds the letter, and as she reads it, she is completely astonished. She is being served and the numbing effect is felt throughout her body. The legal notice informs her that Sam Brown, her husband, is requesting a divorce, custody of Max, and child support from her.

The letter falls out of her hands, as her face turns red, and tears stream down her cheeks. In a mad fury, she struggles to remove her wedding ring, as she silently vows to fight Sam for custody of Max with every ounce of her strength. Caught up in the fury, she considers throwing the wedding ring as hard as she could against the glass wall but hesitates to compose herself. Instead, she tosses it in her desk drawer and slams it shut. Then she looks out at everyone around her, they're busy at work and oblivious to her problems. She's concerned that someone might have noticed her meltdown, but everything on the other side of the glass wall looks peaceful and normal. It's as if nothing has transpired, even though Julie's life has just shattered into a million tiny shards.

She finds it difficult to focus on the space telescope's schematics, as her hostile thoughts are distracting her. She feels the painfulness of this blindside deep in her gut, as she dredges up old memories of hurt and pain from her childhood. She recalls how her parents were so fearful they might ruin her life if they allowed her to make the wrong choices about her education, career and marriage. Then there were the many nights she tossed and turned; afraid she wasn't womanly enough or young enough to keep Sam happy, never bothering to consider if it was him that wasn't worthy of her.

She looks down at her left hand and stares at the spot on her finger vacated by her wedding ring. This is when she realizes that life took her where it wanted her to go, regardless of all her efforts, and carefully considered decisions, she ends up exactly where she supposed to be, so she unfurls the schematics and returns to her work on the Hubble Telescope.

THE END

ABOUT THE AUTHOR

Elyse Wilk is an author, magazine writer, wine collector, and amateur astronomer. A Graduate of Wellesley College with a bachelor's degree in English and Creative Writing and is also an alumna of The International School of Brussels. Lunatics was adapted from her screenplay by the same name.

Her life's greatest battle is with a rare form of Muscular Dystrophy called Myasthenia Gravis, but as long as she and her husband keep laughing all is good.

Made in United States
North Haven, CT
15 January 2025

64043215R00212